totally
Horse
MAD

Kathy Helidoniotis

totally
Horse
MAD

HORSE MAD
1

WALRUS
BOOKS

Walrus Books, an imprint of Whitecap Books

This edition published in North America in 2008 by Whitecap Books Ltd. For
more information, contact Whitecap Books, 351 Lynn Avenue, North Vancouver,
British Columbia, Canada V7J 2C4. Visit our website at www.whitecap.ca.

First published in English in Sydney, Australia by Banana Books, an imprint of
Otford Press, in 2003. This edition is published by arrangement with HarperCollins
Publishers Australia Pty Limited.

The author has asserted their right to be identified as the author of this work.

Library and Archives Canada Cataloguing in Publication

Helidoniotis, Kathy
     Totally horse mad / Kathy Helidoniotis.

(Horse mad series ; 1)
ISBN 978-1-55285-952-0

     1. Horses--Juvenile fiction. I. Title. II. Series: Helidoniotis,
Kathy. Horse mad series ; 1.

PZ7.H374To 2008   j823'.92   C2008-902280-7

The publisher acknowledges the financial support of the Canada Council for the
Arts, the British Columbia Arts Council, and the Government of Canada through
the Book Publishing Industry Development Program (BPIDP). Whitecap Books
also acknowledges the financial support of the Province of British Columbia
through the Book Publishing Tax Credit.

Canada Council Conseil des Arts
for the Arts   du Canada

BRITISH COLUMBIA
ARTS COUNCIL

Printed in Canada.

08 09 10 11 12 5 4 3 2 1

To Mariana, John and Simon
with love

G'day, mate!

This story takes place in Australia — so if you want to brush up on your Aussie slang (what are mozzies?), just flip to the helpful glossary at the back of the book!

ONE

The Dream

I sat up straight in the saddle and patted Princess's firm white neck. She was a champion, the best horse a kid could have and I was here at the Olympics, riding towards a gold medal in the three-day event. I squeezed the mare's middle with my legs, urging her into a trot. The pony moved forward gracefully, her neck arched, her silky tail flying out behind her like a banner. The crowd 'oohed' as we trotted past the grandstand.

There must have been thousands of people watching. They seemed to be as nervous as me. I was, after all, Australia's only chance for a gold medal in the Equestrian event and the competition had been tough. The pressure was enormous. I had to stay in control.

Princess trotted around the arena in a perfect collected pace. She snorted gently with each step. She seemed to be telling me that the medal was in the bag. We were going to be legends before the hour was up. I, Ashleigh Miller, aged just eleven, riding a fourteen-year-old Welsh Cob pony would be the youngest rider ever to win gold at the Olympics.

I nudged Princess into a canter past the judges and prepared myself for the jumps ahead. I was just a minute away from the gold, a minute away from immortality. I would be the girl who had achieved the impossible and snatched victory for her country in the dying minutes of my first Olympics.

The buzzer sounded. I pulled Princess towards the first jump. We were one; one mind and body. Princess tensed as she cantered towards the jump, a parallel spread fence, which seemed taller than a skyscraper. The crowd was silent. The birds were silent. The whole world seemed to have stopped.

I squeezed my legs against her sides at exactly the right moment. Too early and Princess would hit the fence. Too late and she'd hit the fence. I didn't even want to think what would happen to me, but I knew there'd be a big mess for the officials to clean up. I leaned forward and felt Princess lift her head and forelegs. She sprang from her powerful hind legs, sailed over the fence as though she had wings and landed perfectly on the other side. My heart thumped with relief. We'd cleared the first jump. Only a few more jumps, a few more seconds and we would take our place in history ...

'Ashleigh Miller! Wake up from that daydream and concentrate on the job. Princess isn't going to get around those barrels with you in la-la land again.'

I gathered my reins. 'Sorry, Holly.'

My riding instructor, Holly Davis, glared at me from beneath her cowgirl hat. She was mad. Her green eyes were all squashed and her lips had almost disappeared. Even her curls looked stressed. She pointed savagely with her crop at the barrel racing course she'd set up for our four-rider Under 12s team from South Beach Stables.

'Ash, how many times do I have to tell you, don't let your mind wander when you're on horseback!' she snapped. 'What if Princess bolted? What if you missed your event?'

My team-mate Nicki King snorted into her riding gloves. Nicki King is not my favourite person. In fact, if I was ever to write a thesaurus 'Nicki' would be my first listing under the words 'painful', 'spoiled' and 'brat'. I glowered at her. She smiled sweetly at me and brushed imaginary fluff from her immaculate black riding jacket. She thinks she's so great. But expensive riding clothes and indulgent parents aren't everything in my book.

I could see Holly wasn't in the mood to be trifled with. With only a few weeks to go until the most important gymkhana of the year, she didn't need trouble from me.

'Ashleigh, you're rider number four. I'm counting on you. The team is counting on you. Ben's been back at the starting line for at least a minute. The race is over. Stay with me!'

'Okay,' I said, wiping my hands on my old cream jodhpurs. 'I promise I'll concentrate.'

'Sure you won't,' she laughed. I was relieved. 'Now get on with it.'

Holly hated it when I daydreamed. She reckoned I'd cost her a blue ribbon eventually, but I just can't help it sometimes. Horses are my favourite things in the whole world and fantasising about them comes a close second.

I stole a peek at dark-haired, freckled Ben Adams on his horse, the gentle bay gelding, Snow, and Maria Stephanou on Candy, her dapple-grey Welsh Mountain pony, the other two members of the Under 12s. They gave me the thumbs up and grinned. We all knew Holly was the best instructor around, even if she demanded a lot from her riders.

I leaned forward in the saddle, rubbed Princess's mane and breathed in her warm, horsy smell.

'Okay, girl,' I whispered. 'This is it. You know what to do.'

Princess flicked her white ears at the sound of my voice and snorted. We had a good thing going. We were a team. And we both knew that if we didn't turn in a brilliant performance Holly would crack a mental. And Nicki wouldn't be able to wipe the smug look off her face.

I sized up the barrels. This is my favourite event of all. Nothing, not dressage or even jumping, does it for me like getting around those barrels in record time. It's what I live for.

'Get a wriggle on, Ashleigh!' Holly moaned. 'We'll be here till my hundredth birthday.'

'Which isn't all that far away,' Nicki muttered under her breath.

I glared at her, fuming. The only thing I hated about our riding school was riding with Nicki. We'd been stuck together for years.

'Let's go!' I said.

I nudged Princess into a gallop, feeling an instant, delicious rush of speed. We approached the first barrel and I sat deep in the saddle, urging Princess to slow down for the turn. She kept her nose to the barrel as we came around it, close enough to give us a great time, not so close that we knocked it over and were disqualified. Princess took the second like the champion she was. We rounded the third and flew home.

I beamed at Holly who was looking at her watch. She smiled broadly at me. 'Great work, Ash, as usual.'

'Thanks!' I said breathlessly, adrenalin pumping through my veins. Ben and Maria clapped and whistled their approval. Nicki looked like she'd just sucked on a lemon.

'Cool her down, get her gear off and turn her

out,' Holly said, turning to the rest of the Under 12s. 'Same for you lot. You all did great today. I'm sure I can trust you all to take care of your horses while I get ready for the next class.'

'Top ride, Ashleigh,' Ben gushed as we dismounted and walked the horses towards the cool-down arena. 'That was unreal.'

'The best,' Maria agreed.

'Unreal, the best,' Nicki mimicked, fluffing out her cropped strawberry blonde hair with her fingers. 'We'll see how good you look on that old riding school nag next to my new horse.'

I usually did my best to ignore Nicki, but this time I couldn't help myself. A new horse? Nicki had ridden the South Beach horses for as long as I had.

'What new horse?'

'Just the Thoroughbred gelding my parents bought me for my birthday,' she said airily. 'He cost thousands of dollars. And they spent a fortune on a brand new Champion saddle and bridle for me from McWilliam's.' Nicki gave me a slimy look, her eyes gleaming with delight. 'I do believe that McWilliam's is your favourite saddlery, isn't it, Ashleigh?'

Nicki marched away with Ben and Maria hanging on every word she said.

I couldn't believe it.

My guts twisted and my face burned. A Thoroughbred that cost thousands of dollars was being wasted on Nicki.

Later that afternoon I leaned on the fence watching Princess graze and waiting for my ride home. Dad was often late to pick me up from South Beach Stables, with his job and everything. It was okay with me though as I got to spend a few extra moments in my favourite place in the world. Riding lessons once a week just wasn't enough for me. My dream was to ride all day every day.

I'd given Princess a good cool down and a groom and had turned her out into the top paddock. She looked up, nickered to me and ambled across, searching my hands for a titbit. I rubbed her forelock gently. Her eyes drooped with pleasure. She was a great horse. I loved her. We belonged together.

'Holly?' I called from the fence.

Holly looked up from Chelsea's hoof. She was examining the pony's feet for stones on the driveway nearby. 'Yep?'

'How much would a horse like Princess cost?' I asked.

'Princess. Let's see,' she said. She stood up and stretched her back. Her cowgirl hat sat low over her eyes. Chelsea nibbled at strands of grass that poked up between the cracks in the concrete. 'She's an older horse, but she's experienced and she has a great temperament, absolutely bombproof. She's a perfect all-rounder. I reckon we're talking at least eighteen hundred bucks.' She bent down and picked up another of Chelsea's feet. 'Why?'

'Just asking,' I said. But I had a great idea. Maybe I could buy Princess. Then she'd really be mine, not just a horse I rode once a week.

'You'd better not be getting any ideas about Princess, Ash. She's not for sale.'

'Oh.' I was disappointed, but I had made up my mind. If it was the last thing I did, I was going to get my very own horse.

TWO

Horse Cents

There was a knock at the door of our tiny terrace house.

'How was your lesson?' Jenna asked, grinning broadly as I opened the door. (Jenna always grins broadly — her teeth stick out.) Jenna Dawson is my best friend, and only a month older than me. She lives down the street.

'Cool,' I said, stepping out of the way to let her inside. She headed straight for my room and flopped down on the bed.

'It smells in here,' she said, wrinkling her nose.

'Of what?'

'I dunno. The usual smell it gets after you spend a whole entire day hanging around horses.'

'Beautiful, isn't it?'

'Yeah, right!' Jenna rolled over onto her stomach and rested her chin on her hands. 'We've still got a bit of time before dinner. What do you want to do?'

'We could take a walk down to the racetrack,' I suggested. Our street is right near the biggest racecourse in the city.

'Nah.'

'How about we go to the park?'

'You'll only want to hang around the horses again. No thanks.'

'Okay, if you don't want to go out you can at least make yourself useful.'

'How?'

I sat down on the floor, crossed my legs and looked into her eyes.

'Jenna, I need your help.'

'What's wrong?' She sat up quickly.

'Nothing,' I said. 'I have a plan and I need you to help me carry it off.'

Jenna's eyes widened the way they always did when we shared a really good secret. 'Sounds intriguing.'

'I'm going to buy a horse, and I need you to help me come up with some moneymaking ideas.'

'Why don't you just ask your parents again?'

'I asked Dad on the way home,' I said.

'What did he say?'

'Exactly what I expected him to.'

'What, that you can't have a horse because you live in the middle of the city and your backyard is about the same size as a shoebox?'

I shrugged. 'Something along those lines.'

'So why are we having this conversation?' she asked, flicking her long, fair hair over her shoulder.

'Because Dad said *he* wouldn't buy me a horse. He didn't say I couldn't buy one.'

'That's true,' Jenna mused. 'So what do you want me to do?'

'I need ideas!' I said, standing up. I took the horse calendar from my wall and pointed to a date, which I'd circled in thick red texta. 'The annual Southern Zone Gymkhana is on in three weeks.'

'So what?'

'So, wouldn't it be cool if I was riding my own horse by then?'

Jenna frowned. Deep creases appeared above her eyebrows. She always frowns when she's thinking.

'Yes,' she said finally. 'But that's hardly any time to make money. You'll need ...'

'Eighteen hundred bucks,' I finished for her.

Jenna whistled. 'That's a lot.'

'I know, but it's not impossible, not if we do it together. I've already got fifty-three dollars and eighty cents in my moneybox. And I've come up with a great name for my fund, "Horse Cents"!' I grinned, pleased with myself.

'Wouldn't dollars be better than cents?'

Groan. Trust Jenna to miss my fabulous joke.

'Yeah, but "Horse Dollars" just doesn't have the same ring to it.' I held out my hand. 'So, what do you say?'

Jenna leaped off the bed, grabbed my hand. 'I'm in.'

'I've got it all figured out,' I whispered to Jenna during Maths, the next day at school.

Mr Johnson, our teacher, was up at the front raving about percentages. Personally, percentages don't do a lot for me, but he really seems to find them fascinating. I was too busy worrying about the unfunded ninety-seven percent of my horse to even think about percentages.

'You've got what all figured out?' Jenna said through her teeth, staring trance-like at the examples on the whiteboard so that Mr J wouldn't catch us talking.

'How to get Horse Cents off the ground.'

Jenna ruled a red margin down a crisp white page in her Maths book. 'How?'

'I'll get a job. I'll make heaps of money.'

Jenna nodded her approval. I rubbed at the splodge of blue ink that was spreading across my sums and raised my hand.

'Yes, Ashleigh?' Mr Johnson beamed. 'What can I do for you?'

'Can I rub out the board for you, sir?' I asked. 'Only cost you a dollar.'

At lunchtime, Jenna and I sat under a huge old jacaranda tree to eat. It was the best place in the entire school to see the racetrack. You had to climb the tree, of course, and that required precision timing and an eye for the rostered duty teacher. The school oval was crowded with kids playing games.

Soccer balls flew past our heads like squadrons of black and white jets.

'Getting a job sounds like a great idea,' Jenna said as we opened our lunchboxes.

I handed her half of my lunch and accepted a share of hers.

'I've made a list of ideas for Horse Cents,' Jenna said through a mouthful of peanut butter. 'I reckon we'll make heaps.'

She reached into the pocket of her tunic, pulled out a piece of pink paper and cleared her throat. 'One: have a garage sale. Two: collect cans. Three: vacuum lounges. Four: find lost dogs.' She folded up the paper and looked at me intently.

'Jenna, the garage sale I understand and even the lost dogs make sense. But vacuuming lounges?'

'People always lose change behind cushions,' Jenna explained.

'Jenna, you're a genius.'

The school bell rang and we hauled each other to our feet.

THREE

Joy Ride

Ring Two was ready at the annual Southern Districts Gymkhana. Four identical barrel racing courses had been set up on the grass. Judges in long black pants and neat red jackets strode around checking the distances between the bright orange drums with long tape measures. I pulled Princess up at the starting line.

Ben, Maria and Nicki were already there, mounted and ready to go. Holly paced, mumbling under her breath and whacking at her boots with her crop.

'Ashleigh, if Ben can be here on time and Maria can be here on time and Nicki can be here on time,' Holly snapped, 'I see no reason why you can't.'

Nicki shot a smug look in my direction.

'Sorry, Holly,' I said, flushing. 'I just got caught up.'

'Well, make it up to me by setting a world record time around these barrels. Got it?'

'Loud and clear.'

Holly turned to the rest of the team.

'Today is a big day for South Beach Stables. We've got riders competing in most events. We came second overall last year, thanks to the superhuman effort put in by our very own Ashleigh Miller.'

'Fluke,' Nicki muttered, glaring at me. 'Total fluke.'

'Winning is great. But remember, the most important thing is to do your best and have a good time. Ribbons are an added bonus.'

'Going soft in your old age are you, Holly?' Ben laughed. 'Last year you said "Win or else".'

'Must be.' Holly smiled and ducked under the white fence. 'Good luck!'

The Under 12s took up their positions at the starting line.

Ben twisted around in his saddle. 'Just keep your cool, guys, and we'll smash the other teams.'

'So,' said Nicki loudly, 'are your parents going to make it this time, Ashleigh?'

'Of course,' I said, looking past her and out at the arena where hundreds of people sat watching the riders. I really hated Nicki sometimes. She knew exactly what to say if she wanted to upset me. You see, my dad is the best nurse at one of the big city hospitals and my mum's a plumber. Some of my friends think it's weird, but I like it. It makes for interesting dinnertime discussions anyway. But they're always on call and find it hard to get to see me ride. I try to act like it doesn't bother me, but it does. A lot.

'They're better off not wasting their time,' she continued. 'I mean, it's not as if you actually own a horse like we do.'

'Nicki, knock it off,' Ben said, checking out the other teams.

'Personally, I think there should be rules against letting people compete who don't own a horse. I mean, there have to be some standards. They shouldn't just let anyone ride at South Beach.'

'So how'd you slip by?' I snapped as the starting bell rang.

Ben and Snow set off at a gallop. They rounded the first barrel, then the second and the third, and flew home to make a great time.

Nicki was next out. She kicked Sunset hard into a sudden gallop. They neared the first barrel. I waited for Nicki to slow Sunset down for the turn, but she kicked him again and pulled him around hard. Confused, Sunset splayed around the barrel and Nicki lost her seat. My heart leapt.

'Hang on, Nicki!' Maria screamed.

Sensing something was wrong, Sunset stopped dead. Nicki clung to the saddle. For a moment her face was white and her dark eyes wide. She hauled herself up and continued towards the next barrel as though nothing had happened. Although the rest of her ride was clear, the team had lost time.

Maria and Candy galloped out fast and made it around the course in a good time. As they got closer, my heart pounded. I waited for them to dash across the line and urged Princess into a gallop. I felt her sail out beneath me, straight and smooth.

I guided Princess towards the first barrel. As usual, the other riders, the announcers and the cheers from the crowd didn't matter. It was just Princess, the course and me. The barrel loomed ahead. I kept Princess's nose close and she twisted her body around it. She broke away clean and galloped towards the second. We took it faster than the first and aimed for the third. Princess rounded the barrel and galloped for the finish line, her hooves kicking up dust in the faces of the other teams.

I pulled her to a halt and beamed at the rest of the team, breathing hard. Ben cheered and Maria danced in her saddle. Even Nicki was pleased.

'We won, Ash!' Ben yelled.

I dismounted just as Holly rushed over, her curls flying about under her hat. She grabbed me by the shoulders, grinning, and shook me.

'That was one of the best rides I've seen, kid,' she yelled. 'Fantastic. Unbelievable! You were the best. All of you. The best!'

I perched on the bonnet of Holly's car and rubbed the smooth blue ribbon between my fingers. Under-12 Champion, two years in a row.

'Want a lift, Ashleigh?' Maria hung out of the window of her parents' car. Her little brother peeped out from under her riding hat in the back seat.

'No thanks,' I said, pulling my green jacket tight around me. 'Mum and Dad'll be here soon.'

'Okay,' she smiled. 'See you next weekend.' The car pulled away slowly.

Holly was singing nearby ... something about being crazy.

'Can I hose out the float for you, Holly?'

'Sure.'

'Great,' I said, hopping down from the car. 'That'll be five bucks!'

FOUR

Work Horse

'So where did your parents get to?'

'Caught up at work. It was a bad day for exploding pipes and emergency patients.' I examined the notice board in the supermarket. Positions Vacant were advertised on small pieces of yellow cardboard.

'See anything you like?' Jenna squinted up at the board.

'There's a heap of jobs.' I pointed to a card. '*Apprentice panel beater wanted to start immediately.* Or this one: *Pizza deliverers, where are you? Regular work available. Driver's licence required.*'

'Ever driven a car?'

'No.'

'Ever beaten a panel?'

'No.'

Jenna sighed heavily. 'It's no good looking here then. Let's try the shopping centre.'

'Sorry, love, I can't help you.'

A round-faced man smiled over the counter at Harry's Hot Food Bar.

'Come back in a year or two when you're older.' He laughed. 'Maybe three.' Then he turned his back on me and snipped a barbecued chicken right down the middle with a huge pair of scissors.

I met Jenna outside the shop. She smiled at me expectantly. 'Well?'

I shook my head. 'No good. Said I'm underage.'

Jenna picked a long strand of hair from the front of my shirt. 'How far under?'

'Try light years.'

We collapsed together on a bench and rubbed our feet.

'We just might have to face the fact that nobody's gonna give you a job. They've all said the same thing as the barbecued-chook man. All of them.'

I nodded. My horse was slipping further and further out of reach. Something needed to be done.

'Back again?' Emma McWilliam leaned on the counter of McWilliam's Saddlery pulling absent-mindedly at her long ponytail.

'You know I can't get through the week without coming here at least once,' I replied.

'True enough.' She smiled and scribbled something on a piece of paper.

I loved McWilliam's.

I loved the smell of leather and new riding clothes as I climbed the staircase. I loved the rows of brand-new helmets and shiny silver bits that reflected the light. I loved to rub the smooth saddles with my hands and imagine that one of them were mine. I loved everything about the place.

Except Emma's dad, Old McWilliam.

Old McWilliam was sitting at the back of the shop at a tatty desk surrounded by piles of yesterday's newspapers and crusty coffee cups. He examined me through lenses as thick as bottle bottoms from under his bushy grey eyebrows. He was ancient and scary and I always did my best to avoid him.

'Gonna buy something this time, girly?'

I swallowed and backed into a display of videos on mounted games and eventing.

'Just looking.'

Old McWilliam frowned.

'Tell you what. You may as well make yourself useful, instead of just wearing out me floorboards.'

'Who, me?' I said, hoping he meant somebody else.

'Yes.' He nodded. 'You. How'd you like to earn some pocket money?' He creaked out of his chair. I'd never seen him stand before. We were exactly eye to eye.

'Do you mean it?' Could this be true? Old McWilliam was pretty spooky, but he wanted to hire me. Maybe he wasn't that bad.

'I always mean what I say, girly,' he replied.

'I'd love to.'

'I need the back storeroom tidied up. Emma's always up the front at the counter and I'm not much good for that sort of thing any more — it's the bones, girly. They're old. Like me.' He laughed, a loud rasping laugh. 'How does ten dollars sound? Payment on completion, of course.'

I grinned. 'Sounds good.'

He held his hand out. His skin was brown and thin, like sandwich paper. I clasped it. 'It's a deal.'

I reefed open the front door of the house and trudged inside. Dad was dressed in his white hospital uniform sipping coffee at the kitchen table. He looked up at me and smiled.

'You look like you could use a drink.'

'I reckon,' I said, grabbing a carton of blackcurrant juice from the fridge. 'I'm bordering on dehydration.'

I plopped down on a chair, pierced the carton with a straw and sucked down the juice in about two seconds flat.

'Where've you been?' Dad folded up his favourite blue hanky and slipped it into his back pocket.

'Nowhere special.' I shrugged. 'Just up the shops with Jenna. Her dad dropped us off.'

It was then I remembered. Mum and Dad still didn't know about Horse Cents. And I didn't know how happy they'd be about me spending two hours stacking and sweeping in McWilliam's storeroom. I was exhausted. But I had ten dollars in my pocket that hadn't been there in the morning, and Old McWilliam had been a very satisfied customer.

'What for?'

'I was looking for a job.' I picked at the fringe on the tablecloth that Uncle Bill had brought back from his holiday to Egypt.

Dad spluttered into his coffee cup. '*You?*' He was amazed. He wiped at the brown stain that had splattered down the front of his uniform. 'I can't even get you to tidy your room. Why on earth would you be looking for a job?'

'To save up.' I fidgeted with the empty juice carton. The last drops of juice sprayed across the tablecloth like fine pink mist.

'For what?'

This was the moment of truth, his chance to finish Horse Cents before it had even started.

'Just a horse.'

'Exactly how much are we talking about here?'

'About eighteen hundred bucks. Without tack.'

'Oh.' He leaned back into his chair.

'Are you mad?'

'No.' He smiled. 'Actually I'm rather impressed with your initiative.'

'Well, don't be. I couldn't get one.'

'Never mind.' He swallowed the last of his coffee and rinsed the mug out in the sink, turning it upside down to drip dry on the dish rack. 'There's nothing stopping you from doing odd jobs. I made a lot of money when I was your age, washing cars and stuff.'

'You were my age?'

'Yeah, way back in the olden days before electricity.' He laughed and kissed me on the top of my head. He smelled of coffee and aftershave.

'Gotta go, Ash. I'm doing the late shift.'

He gathered up his car keys, checked his reflection in the oven door and left.

'See you,' I called after him.

Dad had just given me another brilliant idea. Odd jobs. Washing cars and stuff. I could handle that.

FIVE

Show Pony

'He's gorgeous!' Maria Stephanou ran her hand along the smooth, firm neck of Nicki King's brand-new horse. The black gelding's withers rippled with pleasure. So did Nicki.

'What's his name?' asked Ben.

'Sonny.'

I felt sick as I watched Holly and the riders of South Beach Stables swarm around Nicki and Sonny like worker bees to their queen. It wasn't fair. Nothing had ever been so totally unfair.

'He's a champion. The best horse anywhere in this city. My parents wanted to make sure I had the top of the line. He cost them a fortune.' Nicki sneered. 'But they said I'm worth it.'

I almost choked.

'Just look at him,' Holly gushed. She took a few steps back and squinted at Sonny. Sonny stood still and obedient like a horse mannequin. 'He's perfect. Calm eyes, pricked ears, neck just the right shape.'

Holly ran her hand down his foreleg. Sonny lifted his foot automatically. 'His foot's great, Nicki.' She stood up grinning.

I'd never seen Holly so worked up about a student's horse before. My stomach pinched with anger. Nicki didn't deserve her own horse. All Nicki cared about was how much he'd cost.

'He's fantastic. Congratulations!' Holly inspected Sonny's other feet. Nicki air-kissed Sonny's perfect face and looked over at me. She waved and turned her attention to the crowd of admirers who had gathered around her. My fists curled up into balls. It was all I could do to stop myself doing something with them I'd regret.

Maria bounded over, smiling. 'What do you reckon, Ashleigh? Is he amazing or what?'

I glared at Nicki, resentment boiling in my stomach, and turned in the direction of the stables. 'He's okay.'

'Just okay? He's unbelievable. Nicki is so lucky.' Maria tramped after me. Our boots scrunched on the gravel driveway.

'Whatever.'

Maria skidded to a halt and put her hands on her hips. 'What's with you? You're like Oscar the Grouch on a bad day.'

'Maybe I'm sick of hearing about Nicki and how lucky she is.'

Maria's face fell. We'd never argued before. Of all the riders at South Beach, I liked her the most. 'I'm sorry,' I said. 'I'm just a bit . . .' I paused, searching for the right word.

'Jealous?'

I looked hard at the ground. I had to admit it, I was jealous of Nicki. My toes were tense inside my boots and my stomach was turning like a ferris wheel. I was so jealous I could taste it. 'Maybe,' I said.

Maria put her arm around my shoulder. 'It must be hard for you. You're the best rider at South

Beach.' She squeezed my hand, her blue eyes looking into mine. 'You'll have a horse soon, too. I just know it.'

We walked towards the stables. 'You don't think there was a baby mix-up at the hospital, do you?' I said.

'What are you talking about?'

'Nicki's parents buy her a horse just like that and I get lumped with the biggest horse-haters in the world. Maybe I was sent home with the wrong people.'

Maria laughed. 'You're a nut.'

I smiled, but I couldn't shake the thought out of my head. I'd seen this kind of thing on the news. It wasn't impossible. I wrote myself a mental note to dig up my birth certificate as soon as I got home.

SIX

Bargains Galore

'Are you for real? Is this only ten dollars?'

A round-bellied middle-aged man held up Dad's framed, autographed photo of Mick Jagger. He pushed the stubby fingers of his other hand through his wild black hair.

'Yep,' I said. 'Ten bucks, just for you. That's the genuine article, too.' I leaned on the kitchen table which Jenna and I had dragged outside once Mum had left for work. It was crammed with dozens of my parents' old things. I'd washed my parents' cars until my hands were raw and looked everywhere for a job without even a nibble. A garage sale was a perfect way to raise money for Horse Cents.

'I know,' he breathed.

'I've been trying to get hold of one of these for donkey's years. Here you go.' He handed me a crumpled ten-dollar bill and embraced Mick Jagger. 'Thanks! I'll tell my friends.'

'We'll make a fortune today,' I declared.

'I still reckon you should sell your own junk,' Jenna said, her blue eyes serious.

I gasped. 'Junk? What do you mean, junk?'

'You know, all that horse stuff.'

'That's not junk! It's very valuable.'

'What about your headless horse clock?'

'It's a timeless piece of equine art.'

'It hasn't worked for years.'

I shook my head. 'No way. My things stay right where they are. Besides, I'm doing my parents a favour getting rid of all this old stuff from the sixties. It's from the last millennium. It's taking up space. You wouldn't believe how many bags I found in the garage. They were probably just going to take them to the tip.'

'Your place *is* small,' Jenna agreed.

'They've never even played these Beatles records,' I said, jabbing a huge stack of flat square sleeves with my finger. 'They're probably worth at least five bucks each. Anyway, everything's on CD now.'

Before long word was out and business was booming. We could hardly keep up with demand. People seemed to find our street by magic and were overjoyed to find so many bargains. Within an hour we had over a hundred dollars.

'How much do you want for this dress? It's really quite exquisite. Is it real silk?' A young woman sporting an enormous sparkly rock on her ring finger ran her hands over one of Mum's old dresses, dreamy eyed.

Jenna did a quick valuation. 'For you, fifteen bucks.'

'Sold!' she slapped the money down on the table and hurried away with her purchase.

I counted my money again and again: one hundred and fifty-five dollars. I had never held so much money in my entire life and my horse seemed closer now than it ever had before.

'Excuse me,' said a voice, which sounded kind of familiar.

'Just a minute, please,' I said. 'Jenna, would you just stick this on Dad's guitar?' I passed her a white sticky label.

'*Reduced to $10.* That's a bargain, Ash!'

'Excuse me,' the voice repeated.

'What can I do for you?' I looked up at a very angry-looking man whose face was almost the same colour as his hair. 'Dad!' I gasped. 'What are you doing home so early?'

His mouth opened and closed a few times, but for once in his life he didn't seem able to speak. This was a miracle. I come from a long line of talkers, and he's one of them. His face had changed from deep red to the colour of woodwork glue.

'Dad, what's wrong?' I asked.

He made a strange choking sound.

A few people backed away from him as though they were afraid he might explode.

'Dad,' I hissed. 'You're scaring our customers away.'

'How much, love?' said a tough-looking young man holding up Dad's old leather motorbike jacket. *Bikes* was tattooed across his knuckles, one letter on each.

Dad snatched the jacket. His eyes were as round and red as pizzas.

'I worked every day for six months to save up the money for this jacket,' he said, running his hands

36

over the smooth black leather. 'I wore this on the first date I ever had with your mother.'

Surely, I thought, he'd be glad to unload something so out of fashion. I looked at Jenna. Jenna looked at the sky.

'I want to buy this jacket,' the tough guy said, grabbing hold of a fistful of leather. 'At twelve dollars it's a steal. Go get your own.'

That's when things got ugly.

'This *is* my own!' Dad roared, ripping the jacket out of the man's grip.

People stopped dead and stared at him. He spun around and faced them. 'Now get out, all of you!'

'Well, really,' said a blue-haired old lady. 'How rude.' She put down Mum's tiara and shuffled down the driveway with my other customers.

My garage sale was well and truly over.

Dad looked from me to Jenna and spoke through the thinnest lips I have ever seen. 'Jenna, I think you should go home now. Ashleigh Louise and I have something to discuss.'

My heart pounded with fear. I only ever get called *that* when I'm in big trouble.

Jenna untied her dad's *Kiss the Cook* apron, gave me a sympathetic smile, and took off down the street for the safety of home.

Now there was just me and Dad.

He looked at me. His eyes half-closed. His face was red again. His right cheek made slight twitching movements. I had never seen him so angry before. He was about to give Mount Vesuvius a run for its money.

SEVEN

Big News

'Long time no see, Ashleigh. Come in!'

Jenna's dad held the door open. The smell of freshly baked biscuits washed over me.

'I've just taken some bikkies out of the oven. Chocolate chip.'

'Yum!' I followed him through to the kitchen, my mouth watering. Jenna's dad makes the best chocolate chip biscuits I've ever tasted.

'Here.' He passed me a warm one right off the cooling rack. 'You can be my taste-tester for today.'

'A dollar a taste.'

'Nice try.'

I nibbled on the crunchy brown biscuit. 'Thanks, it's delicious.'

'Jenna's in her room. Go on through.'

Jenna was playing with her computer and her blue eyes lit up when I walked in. It was the first time we'd been able to get together outside school for two weeks.

'Hi,' she said, 'this is a surprise. You haven't been here since you were grounded.'

'The longest two weeks of my life. I only made parole yesterday after lunch.' I sat down on her bed and kicked off my joggers.

Jenna smiled. 'How's it going?'

I sighed. 'I've got the worst case of indigestion in medical history.'

'Indigestion?' Jenna raised her eyebrows. 'How come?'

'I've had to swallow the word "horse" at least a thousand times since my sentencing. It's a banned word at my place now. But worst of all . . .'

'Wait,' Jenna said. 'I'll shut the door.'

She closed her bedroom door and sat at my feet.

'I had another one of those ideas,' I said. 'You know, the brilliant kind.'

'Uh huh.' Jenna had a knowing look in her eyes.

'I decided that the best thing to do with Horse Cents was to bet it on a race.'

'What?' Jenna gasped. 'You can't be serious.'

I nodded. 'I am. As soon as my sentence was lifted I went to the TAB with all my money, all sixty-eight dollars and eighty cents and . . .'

'Hang on, you made heaps at that garage sale,' Jenna interrupted.

I sighed. 'I had to give it all back, remember? I told you at school.'

Jenna smiled sheepishly. 'Oh yeah. Then what happened?'

'Just as I was about to be served Dad busted me. He went totally off his brain.'

Jenna's eyes were wide. 'What did he say?'

'What didn't he say, more like. I was *forbidden on pain of death to ever set foot inside another gambling establishment.*' I mimicked my father and shook my finger at Jenna.

'I can't believe he didn't ground you for the rest of your life!'

'He said he's already suffered enough. He reckons he'll be committed to an institution for desperate dads if he spends one more day watching me mope around the place.'

She fell about on the floor laughing. 'You are a real head case!'

When I got home I found Mum in the kitchen. She was chopping vegetables for dinner, singing her head off and using a large eggplant as a microphone. She was so absorbed in her performance that she didn't notice me coming in. I leaned on the table, arms folded, then gave her an enthusiastic round of applause.

'Bravo! No encore, no encore!'

She turned a strange plum colour and resumed chopping.

'How long have you been there?'

'Too long.' I opened the fridge, grabbed some carrot sticks and munched. 'Can I peel the potatoes?'

Mum smiled. She looked surprised. 'Of course you can. That's very thoughtful.'

'No problem. Fifty cents each.'

'I thought as much.' The smile vanished.

'That's a bargain,' I said, reaching for a fat dirty

potato. 'And for only fifty cents extra I'll chop them up for you.'

'I've got some news for you, Ash,' she said, laying down her knife.

'Oh, yeah? What is it?' For a minute I expected her to tell me that Dad had decided to lock me up again after all. I snatched another carrot and crunched.

'How would you feel if I said that you could have a horse?'

I gaped at her thinking this must be a joke. I looked around expecting one of those practical joke television show hosts to jump out from behind the fridge.

I searched Mum's brown eyes and realised that she wasn't kidding. Then the real meaning of what she had said dawned on me.

How would I feel? I switched on my mental thesaurus and searched for an appropriate word.

'I'd be stoked!' I said, grinning, bits of carrot stuck between my teeth.

Mum picked up her knife from the chopping board and reached for an onion. 'Well, prepare to be stoked. You're going to have a horse!'

'Really?'

'Really,' she said.

'All my very own?'

'All your very own.'

'But, how? Why?'

I dropped my carrot and grabbed Mum by the hands, twirling her around the kitchen and laughing like a lunatic. We crashed into a chair and collapsed on the ground, panting hard.

'Dad's found a new job,' she said, picking herself up. 'We're moving to the country in two weeks.'

For a minute, I didn't think I'd heard her correctly. I thought she'd said that we were moving to the country, but that couldn't possibly be true. Mum is always telling me I never listen properly. Selective deafness I think she calls it. I stuck a finger in each ear and wriggled them around just to make sure the canals weren't obstructed.

'Did you just say we're moving?'

Mum regarded me for a moment. 'What's the matter with you, Ashleigh? I thought you wanted a horse.'

'I do, but do we have to move?'

'Where on earth can we keep a horse around here?'

'City Stables. It's right across the park.'

Mum shook her head. 'It costs a fortune. And besides, your dad and I have always wanted to live in the country. Peace and quiet, fresh air, chooks, it's always been our dream.' Her eyes looked all faraway and misty.

'But where will we live?'

'We bought a house, a big beautiful house. In a town called Shady Creek.'

'When?' I said, shock sinking to the pit of my stomach.

'A few weeks ago. You've been so wrapped up in your fundraising you never noticed. And you remember those times Dad was late to pick you up?' I nodded. 'He was down inspecting the new place. It's a long drive.'

'But why didn't you tell me before this?' A sticky lump was lodged in my throat. 'How could you keep this a secret?'

'Oh, Ash,' Mum sighed. 'We didn't want to get your hopes up if we weren't sure. Buying a house isn't like buying a pair of shoes. It's complicated. It takes time.'

'But what about our house here in the city?'

'It's on the market.'

That meant someone else was going to live here. Someone else was going to sleep in my room and eat here in my kitchen and soak in my bathtub. I'd lived in here since I was born. I didn't want to live anywhere else.

'But what about school?'

'There's a lovely little school in Shady Creek. We would never have considered the move if the school wasn't every bit as good as your school here.'

'But what about your job at Mick's Master Plumbers?'

'I resigned. I'll get another job. There are heaps of toilets in the country, you know.' She smiled.

'But,' I gulped, not sure I wanted to hear the words. 'But what about Princess and South Beach and Holly? I won't ride there any more, will I?'

Mum's face softened and she tucked a loose wisp of dark hair behind my ear. 'No, possum. You won't.'

I didn't feel stoked any more.

'Come sit with me,' Mum said. We sat at the kitchen table. Hot tears stung my eyes. I fought them back. 'Ashleigh, I know this is really big news, but just think. We're moving to the country. There are squillions of horses in the country. We've bought a real house with five acres. There's even a stable.'

'A stable?'

She nodded. 'A stable. You'll get your horse. I promise.'

I gave her a tentative smile. 'Do you really mean it?'

'Hundred percent.'

'My horse,' I whispered.

I looked at Mum. She nodded, grinning. I hadn't seen her look this excited ever. Not even when she won Plumber of the Year.

'Are you happy?' she asked.

I imagined a horse of my own in a stable of my own and days, years of riding any time I wanted. Paradise.

I beamed at her. 'Yes. Definitely, yes. I can't wait to tell Jenna.'

EIGHT

Bombshells

'Come again?' Jenna stared at me. Her blue eyes were as round as doughnuts.

'We're moving,' I said. 'Dad's starting his new job in two weeks.'

'Are you serious?' Jenna half-smiled at me, expecting me to start rolling around on the grass laughing and saying, 'Fooled you!' But April the first was months away.

'I sure am,' I said. 'Mum and Dad have bought a big old homestead on five acres in this little town. They showed me photos of it last night. There's a barn and a stable and I'll have a humungous room of my own. It's got a walk-in wardrobe for all my riding clothes.'

Jenna glowered at her tuna roll.

'And guess what else?' I said. 'It's finally going to happen. They're going to buy me a horse.' I laughed aloud with pleasure and took another bite of my sandwich.

Jenna glanced at me, then wrapped up her roll and crammed it, uneaten, into her lunchbox.

'I'm so excited. Now I'll have to start going to auctions and looking in the paper for real. I don't think I'll be able to choose.'

Jenna sat still and quiet, watching the lunchtime soccer balls zoom around the oval like meteors.

I took a long suck of chocolate milk and grinned at her. 'You'll have to help me choose a horse. There are heaps of breeds. Just look at this.' I pulled a copy of *Horse and Pony Trader* out of my school bag and leafed through it. 'There are Welsh Cobs and Hackneys. Check this one out, Jen, this orange horse. It's called a Halflinger. It can live for forty years! They're either chestnut or palomino.'

Jenna clucked her tongue.

'Which is your favourite? There are bays and duns and dapple-greys. Then there are the markings. I love stars the best, but stripes look good too.'

I slurped down the last of my milk and beamed at Jenna. Something looked strange. Her face was cold. She stared right through me. And she hadn't said a word. 'What's wrong? Are you sick? Are your allergies acting up? What is it?'

Jenna's eyes were red. She shook her head and sniffled. 'You just don't get it, do you?'

'Don't get what?' I said. I'd never seen her like this before.

'You'll be leaving me.'

I chewed on my thumbnail. I was so excited about the move and my horse, I thought she'd be as happy as I was. 'But I'm getting a horse,' I said weakly. 'They promised.'

'Who cares about a dumb old horse?' Jenna said. Her eyes were wet with tears.

'I thought you did.' My heart pumped.

Jenna zipped up her bag and leapt to her feet. 'News flash, Ashleigh. I don't. I never did. I just pretended this whole time.'

'But what about Horse Cents?' I scrambled to my feet.

'You know what you can do with Horse Cents?

You can shove it. I'm over it. I'm over the whole thing.'

I reached out to her. 'Jenna, please, try to understand.'

Jenna pushed me away. 'If horses are more important to you than your friends, you can drop dead, Ashleigh!' she shrieked. 'I hate you. I am *never* talking to you again!'

NINE

Goodbyes

I leaned over the wall of Princess's stall and stroked her face.

'I can't believe I'm leaving you,' I murmured.

Princess gazed at me with gentle brown eyes. I wanted to cry.

The past few days had been the hardest of my life. Packing all my things into boxes, seeing my room almost bare, saying goodbye to Mr Johnson and my friends at school, knowing that I would never see them again — it had all been terrible. I'd used up boxes of tissues. Especially as Jenna and I still hadn't made up. (It hurt so much to think about her.) But although Jenna was my best friend, saying goodbye to Princess was the worst of all. We were a team. I had promised her I'd never give her up, but here I was saying goodbye. I felt like a traitor.

I kissed her nose and rubbed my fingers under her chin. 'I'm going to miss you, girl.'

'She'll be in safe hands,' Holly said, putting her arm around my shoulder.

I jumped. 'You scared me.'

The truth was, I was glad of the company. I needed a distraction. I didn't want to cry in front of Princess.

'Jittery?' Holly hooked her thumbs into her belt and gave me a weak smile.

I nodded. 'I'm so scared.'

'You'll be fine. Moving somewhere new is scary. But it's nothing you can't handle — just another challenge. And you'll meet it the way you ride Princess. With guts and enthusiasm.'

'But I'll be alone. I won't know anyone. What if they hate me? What if I hate it there?'

Holly bit her bottom lip, thinking. 'You'll make it, Ash. I know you will.'

I tried to perk up a bit, for Holly, but I still felt bad. Shady Creek was so far away. I'd be alone, without Jenna for the first time in my life. And without Princess. What if she forgot about me? What if they both did?

I turned back to Princess and rubbed behind her ears. Holly seemed to be reading my mind.

'She'll miss you, Ash. But don't worry. I'll make sure she gets heaps of TLC.'

'Make sure her new rider loves her and treats her right and gives her loads of apples.' My voice wavered. I knew the tears were coming whether I wanted them to or not.

'Leave it to me.' Holly walked away. 'I don't know what I'm going to do without you, kid. This place won't be the same.' She blew her nose and disappeared around the corner.

'It'll be better.'

I spun around. Nicki King stood in the open door of the stables, hands on her hips.

'Which school did you say you'd be riding for? Hicksville Stables, wasn't it?' She turned on her heel and marched away.

'I'll miss you, Nicki!' I called after her.

'Not,' said Ben, laughing.

Ben and Maria were standing nearby. Maria seemed to be hiding something behind her back.

'We just wanted to say goodbye and wish you luck,' Maria said.

'And that we hope you get your horse soon!'

'Thanks.' I smiled at them, not knowing what to say. I was going to miss them so much.

'We'll leave you two alone,' said Ben, indicating Princess. 'But before we do there's something we wanted to give you.'

Maria pulled a package from behind her back.

'For you!'

She stuffed it into my hands.

'Thanks!' I stammered. 'Thanks a lot.'

I stared at the package, which was wrapped in gold paper with silver horseshoes stamped all over it.

'Open it!' Ben urged.

I ripped the paper away.

'Look,' Maria said before I had a chance to speak. 'A photo album. There are heaps of pictures of you and Princess at the gymkhana. My mum took those.' She flicked through the pages. 'And there's us two together and Ben and Holly and even Nicki!'

'We thought you'd like something to remember her by.'

'Thanks, Ben, but I've got enough Nicki memories for a lifetime of nightmares,' I said, rubbing at my eyes with the back of my hand.

'And one of Princess's shoes. I polished it up for you,' Ben said, smiling.

'And that ribbon is from Holly,' Maria added. Her eyes were glistening. 'It's from her collection.'

I hugged them both, hard. 'What am I gonna do without you?' I whispered.

Maria blinked her eyes as a tear rolled down her cheek. 'What are *we* gonna do without *you*? Now it's just us and Nicki!'

'Ashleigh!' Holly called from outside. 'Your mum's here.'

'Goodbye, Ash,' Maria said, dragging Ben out by the arm.

I waved to them, too upset to speak. Princess nudged my shoulder with her nose and I threw my arms around her neck. I buried my face in her sleek, white coat and felt her warmth for the last time. I couldn't believe this was it. I guess, deep down, I'd always wanted her to be mine. It had sure felt like she was mine. I knew Holly owned Princess, but nobody knew her and loved her like I did. I rubbed my face into her coat, smelling her sweetness. My throat felt hot and tight.

'Goodbye, Princess,' I whispered. 'Don't forget me.'

I tore myself away from her and ran to the car, without looking back, warm tears spilling down my face. Without Jenna and Princess the world I knew was lost forever.

TEN

Paradise

'*Welcome to Shady Creek: population 735.* Does that include us?'

'I've got absolutely no idea,' Dad said, stretching in the passenger seat.

'Where do I turn, Grant?' Mum looked from side to side and slowed the car to a crawl. She's always nervous driving somewhere new, but it gave me time to check out all the places where I could go riding.

'Just ahead, Helen. First left.' Dad wound down the window and stuck his face outside like a dog. 'Just breathe that fresh country air, Ashleigh. You'll be as tall as a giraffe before the year is out.'

I pressed my nose against the glass and examined my new town. Little clouds of steam formed around my nostrils. I wiped them away with my sleeve.

There were lush green paddocks, dotted with homes, on both sides of the road. They stretched back to a dark mountain behind us and as far as I could see in front. Cottony white balls of cloud waltzed across the sky.

'Oh, it's breathtaking,' Mum gasped.

'Are there any horses here?' I strained to see out of the driver's side window. 'I need to assess the Shady Creek horse population and its characteristics.'

Dad peered into the back seat at me and raised his ginger eyebrows. 'We're in the country. There's bound to be a few.'

'Over there!' I yelled.

Mum jammed on the brakes. 'What is it?'

'Five horses.'

Mum shifted the car into first gear and exhaled. 'You nearly gave me a heart attack. I thought I was about to drive over a kangaroo or something.'

We drove past Shady Creek Shopping Centre. There were a dozen shops, a Chinese restaurant, a petrol station and a Co-op Store. I took special note of the Co-op. I had to know where to buy feed for my horse. Shady Creek Primary School was right next door to the shops.

'Look, Ash.' Dad tapped on the window. 'Your new school. You'll be starting there in a few days.'

'Oh.' I tried to swallow what seemed to be a big sticky marshmallow that had suddenly become stuck in my throat.

'Here, Helen,' said Dad about five minutes later.

Mum stopped the car in the middle of a long thin road.

'Well, this is it, Ashleigh. Our new place.' Dad pointed to a double-storey house that sat at the end of a long driveway. It was surrounded by lush green pasture and edged by a tall timber fence.

'That's our house? I don't believe it. The driveway is longer than our old street!'

'That's not all, kiddo.' Dad's blue eyes glowed. 'There's five acres of land, a stable, a tack shed, four fenced-off paddocks, a corral and ...' he trumpeted through his scrunched-up fist as though he was about to do a magic trick '... a pool!'

My mouth dropped open. 'No way.'

'Yes way.'

Mum burst into tears. 'Isn't it beautiful?'

My parents exchanged a soppy smile and touched fingertips. I bounced in the back seat. 'So what are we waiting for?'

We drove at snail pace down the driveway towards the house. There was a long fence on each side of the drive and behind it, a paddock. One was cleared and flat, perfect for jumping and eventing practice. On the far side of that paddock was a similar-looking house to ours with a corral at the back and its own equally grassy paddocks. On the other side was a huge green paddock, for grazing and resting my horse, with trees, heaps of grass and a dam. 'I must be dreaming,' I whispered to myself. 'This can't be ours.'

We pulled up in front of the house and tumbled out of the car.

'Oh Grant,' Mum cried. 'Leadlight windows. I've always wanted leadlight windows.'

'Look, a wrap-around veranda. We can get a hammock. Won't it be great?' Dad swept Mum into his arms.

I couldn't take any more of their soppiness. I wanted to check out the important bits, like where my horse would live.

Nestled behind the house was a pool. A real in-ground pool, and behind it was a corral with a tack shed and a stable. There were no cars, no planes and no neighbours an arm's reach from your bedroom window. Just birds chirping, cows mooing and the distant sound of horses whinnying to one another.

I turned and raced back out the front to tell Mum everything I'd seen and stopped dead in my tracks.

Horses! There were horses loping past our gate, at least a dozen of them, one after the other. Their riders were talking and laughing with each other, all dressed in identical uniforms. I took one look at my parents waltzing along their wrap-around veranda gazing into one another's eyes like lovesick teenagers and jogged down the driveway. I had to find out where the horses were going.

ELEVEN

Thrills and Spills

I stood in front of the sign reading it over and over.

'Shady Creek Riding Club,' I said to a small blue heeler that sat panting in the shade of the fence. 'Can you believe I live on the same street as Shady Creek Riding Club?'

The dog, overwhelmed by my news, collapsed in a dusty heap and fell asleep.

I had followed the horses to a huge paddock, a hundred metres down the road. There was a rough-looking arena, an old red-brick office, a log corral and a rusty iron shed scattered along the white timber fence. It was nothing like South Beach, which had the best, brand-new facilities in the city, but I couldn't have cared. There was a real riding club on my street. It didn't get any better than that. The rest of the paddock stretched out in front of me and promised excellent riding; as soon as I got my horse.

There were nearly twenty horses: bays, duns, dapple-greys, roans, a pure white pony just like Princess and a black gelding with a perfect white star on his forehead, all tethered quietly in the corral.

The riders were resting on the grass in the invitingly cool shade of a gum tree. I slid through a gap in the fence and walked over to them.

'Hi,' I called.

'Hey there!' A boy with a shock of wild brown hair that looked like a rat's nest, sat up and grinned at me. The others pretended I wasn't there.

'Would you mind if I pat your horse?' I wiped my hands down my pants.

'Like horses, do ya?' Rat's Nest knocked his shiny black boots together. I noticed he had huge silver Western-style spurs buckled onto them.

'Yeah.' I took a step closer. 'I do. Heaps.'

'Do you know how to ride?' Rat's Nest stood up,

brushed the bits of dry grass from his jodhpurs and stepped into the sunlight. His blue club jumper was tied around his waist, the sleeves hanging down limply like cooked fettuccine.

'Of course,' I said, smiling at the rest of the group. 'I was Under-Twelve Champion the last two years in a row back home.' They squinted up at me from beneath their helmets and grinned. I noticed a pair of identical twin girls who looked a little younger than me.

'How about a ride on my horse?' he said. 'His name's Scud.'

I heard muffled laughter from the group. The twins sat close together, deep in whispered conversation. One of them pointed at me and frowned.

'Really?'

'No worries.'

A pretty girl stood up, smiling. Her red hair was swept back into a neat bun and decorated with a dark blue ribbon. Her uniform was perfect. *Shady Creek Riding Club* was embroidered on her shirt in elegant gold letters. She unbuckled her helmet and passed it to me. 'Here. You'll need this.'

I accepted the helmet. 'Thanks. Mine's still in the boot of the car.'

'Are y'comin'?' Rat's Nest loped over to the black gelding with the white star.

'What's your name?' I said, following him.

'Everyone calls me Flea.'

Flea untied Scud's soft leather reins from a slipknot woven through a piece of twine, which was attached to a thick post in a corner of the corral. He handed them to me. I ran my hand over Scud's sleek black neck.

'He's beautiful. You're so lucky.'

'Do you have a horse?'

I shook my head. 'Not yet. But I'm getting one soon. That's why we moved here.'

'You can't join the club without one.' Flea offered me a leg-up.

I gathered the reins to the right of Scud's withers and prepared to mount. Encouraged by Flea's broad smile I placed my foot in his hands, clasped the pommel and sprang into the saddle.

I settled into the soft, worn stock saddle and beamed, looking over at the group, who were watching me. The twins got up and hurried over.

'Comfy?' asked Flea.

'Sure am,' I said. 'I was born on horseback.'

'Take him for a spin.'

I nodded and gathered the soft leather reins, passing them carefully between my fourth and little fingers. I held them with my thumbs and let the loop fall down towards Scud's left shoulder. Holly would have been proud.

'Wait!' One of the twins grabbed the reins near Scud's bit. Her long dark braid was tied with a red ribbon.

'What do ya think you're doin', Julie?' said Flea, his voice laced with menace.

The other twin tapped my knee. She looked exactly like her sister, right down to the braid, except her ribbon was blue. 'You really shouldn't ride Scud,' she said.

I looked at Flea, puzzled.

Flea peeled Julie's fingers from the reins. 'Just go away,' he hissed. 'You too, Jodie.'

Jodie with the blue ribbon shook my leg. 'It's not a good idea ...' she began.

'What's going on?' I said. The twins chewed on their bottom lips.

Flea nudged Jodie with his elbow. 'Let the girl ride, will ya?'

'You're not a member,' she continued, grabbing the reins under Scud's chin. 'Gary wouldn't like it.'

'It's okay,' I assured her. 'I'm very experienced.'

Flea smiled and led Scud out of the corral into the open paddock. The twins stood together and watched, shaking their heads in perfect unison.

'Go for it,' Flea said, stepping back a little.

I squeezed both of Scud's dark flanks equally with my legs and held my hands level above his withers. Nothing happened. I checked the length of the stirrups; they were fine. I squeezed again, using a bit more pressure. Scud remained still.

I couldn't understand what was wrong. My technique had never failed on Princess, or Pepper, the first horse I had ridden at South Beach. My seat was perfect. I could draw an imaginary line from my shoulder to my hip and down to my heel. My wrists were supple and straight. My head was up. My knees were in firm contact with the saddle, and my feet were parallel to the ground. I was doing everything right.

I squeezed Scud's sides again and when he didn't

react I nudged him with my heels. The members of Shady Creek Riding Club had scrambled away from their patch of grass under the gum tree and perched themselves on the fence. They were chattering to each other, watching every move I made.

I looked at Flea in disbelief. 'What's wrong with him?'

'He just needs a bit of encouragement.'

With that he brought his open hand down on Scud's round rump with an ear-splitting slap.

Scud exploded into a bolt, tearing like a lunatic across the paddock. I was so utterly shocked, for a moment I couldn't think. What was I doing here? One minute I was running down my new driveway, the next I was hanging onto the neck of a crazy horse for dear life. Once my brain was working again, I tried to remember everything Holly had taught me about what to do during a bolt. There was only one small problem. Princess, and certainly old Pepper, had never ever bolted. This was my very first time and I was so scared. I tried to turn him in a large circle and leaned back in the saddle. I held on to the pommel, sinking my heels deep into the stirrups and pulling back on the reins. Scud didn't react. I tried it over and over again, but he refused to stop.

My heart thumped and blood roared in my ears. I heard screaming and realised it was me. The sound of my own screams and Scud's hooves on the hard-packed earth and the shouts of the riders frightened me even more. For the first time ever, I was terrified on horseback.

But I tried to stay calm, the sensible part of my head telling me that he wouldn't intentionally hurt himself. If I could just manage to stay in the saddle until he got bored with the whole thing I'd be okay. I gripped so hard with my knees that my thighs hurt. They clung to the saddle.

Suddenly, fed up with just galloping around like a lunatic, Scud bucked, swerved and thrashed until with one enormous pig-root he sent me flying, SPLAT, into the biggest, prickliest blackberry bush he could find. Then he came to a dead stop, grazing calmly on the grass as though nothing had happened.

I lay there for a while, gasping for breath, feeling pain in every single part of my body, including some parts I hadn't been aware of before. My legs hurt, my back hurt, my elbows hurt. Even my belly button hurt.

I hauled myself to my feet, limped across to Scud and checked him over, trying to ignore the agonising feeling in my bum and the shame of having been thrown in front of the very people I had hoped would be my new friends. Scud was sweaty, but unhurt. I slipped the reins over his head and led him back to Flea.

He grinned. 'You okay?'

I handed him his reins. 'Well, apart from the blood pouring out of my elbow and the blackberry bush spikes that I'll be pulling out of my butt until my twenty-first birthday, I'm fine.'

Flea roared with laughter.

'You set me up,' I yelled. 'How could you do that?'

'Don't forget,' Flea spluttered. 'You're very ex–per–ienced.'

The pretty girl who'd loaned me her helmet staggered forward, bent double with laughter. She didn't look so pretty now, though. 'Yeah, Under-Twelve Champion. What a joke!'

I glared at them, looking from one face to another. The twins stared at me with solemn eyes.

'We tried to stop you,' Twin Julie with the red ribbon mumbled.

Hot tears of hurt and humiliation pricked behind my eyes. Just as I was ready to tell the members of Shady Creek Riding Club exactly what I thought of them a booming voice stopped me dead in my tracks.

'Would somebody mind telling me what on earth is going on here?'

TWELVE

Shady Creek Riding Club

'Inspection, now!' A man mounted on a pinto mare boomed at the members of Shady Creek Riding Club.

He was with a dark-eyed girl, who was riding a beautiful bay gelding with a white blaze and four white socks. She seemed to be about the same age as me. Her hair was twisted into a thick black plait that tumbled down her back almost to her waist, tied at the end with a blue ribbon to match her club jumper. She looked at me coolly for a moment, then stared across the paddock.

The riders burst into action, jogging to the corral and untying their horses. Within a few minutes every rider except Flea was mounted on a horse and lined up into groups of five on the arena, ready for inspection.

'So, what's been happening here?'

'Nothing,' Flea said. 'We were just getting to know ... um ...'

'Ashleigh. Ashleigh Miller,' I said, unbuckling the pretty girl's helmet. 'I just moved in down the street.'

'Yeah,' Flea grinned, taking the helmet. 'Right next door to me.' He sprang into his saddle and took his place in line with the other riders.

I remembered the house with the corral out the back and my heart drooped. It was just my luck. First I'd been thrown within an inch of my life. Now I'd discovered I'd be sharing a fence with a kid who looked like he had a rodent stuck to his head. Shady Creek was starting to look less and less like paradise with every passing minute.

The man smiled down at me. 'I'm Gary Cho, the instructor here at Shady Creek Riding Club. This is my daughter, Rebecca.' He indicated the girl on the bay gelding.

She blushed. '*Becky*, Dad. Not Rebecca.'

'Okay, okay. Becky.' He held his hands up in a sign of surrender.

Becky joined her group for inspection. None of the other riders seemed to notice that she was there. But I was beginning to learn that not everything was as it first appeared in Shady Creek.

'You all right?' Gary said, staring at the blood that was drying on my arm.

'It's nothing. I just tripped on my shoelace. It doesn't even hurt.' That wasn't true. It hurt a lot, and if I hadn't been feeling so queasy I'd have had a really good look at it to see just how many stones were stuck in my elbow.

'Is it okay if I hang around for a while?'

'Sure,' he said as he hurried over to inspect the riders. 'You can help me out with the equipment later if you want.'

'Really?'

'We'll begin with a gear and safety check as usual,' Gary called to the riders. 'Keep your horses settled in your groups until you're cleared. I'd like to introduce you to Miss Ashleigh Miller. She'll be helping out today.'

'We've met,' the pretty girl who'd loaned me her helmet said, smiling. She was mounted on the pure white pony I had seen tethered in the corral. 'She's a great rider.'

My face burned with anger. Some of the riders laughed.

'We'll start on the left and work our way across to the right,' Gary said, passing me a folder and a pen. 'I'll check the gear and uniforms and you tick off on the page, okay?'

I nodded and opened the folder. The helmet owner leaned forward and patted her pony's neck.

'Being Gary's secretary? You must be some rider, Ashleigh.'

'This is Carly Barnes and her horse Destiny,' Gary said suddenly. Had he heard? I wasn't sure. 'Carly is one of our best riders. She did very well in dressage at last year's Zone Gymkhana.'

'I can't stand dressage,' I said, ticking items off under Carly's name in red pen.

Carly sucked in her breath, her dark eyes flashing with anger. 'At least I have a horse. At least I'm not following Gary around with a folder.' She gave me a look that let me know exactly what she thought of the newest member-to-be of Shady Creek Riding Club.

'Everybody's clear,' Gary called. 'I'd like to see a warm-up for at least ten minutes, starting at a walk and finishing with a nice, smooth canter. Stick to the arena, no haring around the paddock. Right, Flea?'

'Aye, aye, Captain.' Flea saluted Gary and kicked Scud into a walk, clockwise around the arena. Carly and a kid called Ryan on Arnie, his stocky grey quarter horse joined him.

I watched them warm up their horses. They were okay riders. But after a while Becky Cho on her bay Welsh-Arab gelding, Charlie, stood out more than the others. She was a great rider, smooth and graceful. She seemed to be a part of her horse.

'That was a good warm-up,' Gary called to the riders. 'How about some games?'

Jodie and Julie cheered and Carly smiled. Flea and Ryan high-fived each other. But Becky's face was blank, like a mask. I realised that the whole time I'd been watching her ride I hadn't seen her smile once. There was something definitely weird about that. I mean, how could anyone ride a horse as fantastic as Charlie and not crack even a tiny smile? If I were her, I thought, I'd be smiling so huge my jaws would ache.

'We'll start with some witches' hats. I want you to take them through at a walk, starting on the left side and weaving in and out until you reach the last hat. Turn right around and make your way back through the hats. Got that?'

There were nods all round.

'Okay, Reb ... um Becky, you start off. Then Ryan, Carly and everyone else.' Gary smiled at the riders and pulled his cap lower over his eyes.

'Typical,' Flea sneered under his breath, scratching the back of his head. 'Becky always goes first.'

Carly tossed her head. 'I'd be going first too if *my* daddy was the instructor.'

So that was it. No wonder Becky looked miserable.

Becky stared straight ahead at the course pretending not to have heard and walked Charlie through it. The rest of the riders followed suit.

Gary applauded. 'That was perfect. You all did well.'

'It wasn't exactly hard, Gary. We were only walking,' Carly said, fidgeting with the dark blue ribbon that was tied around her bun.

'Maybe so, Carly. But we always start with the basics. Repeat the course, this time at a trot, then a canter. Start on the left again and go right around the last hat, same as before.' Gary looked at Carly. 'You first this time for group one.'

Carly looked pleased. She gathered her reins and urged Destiny into a trot. They completed the course and rejoined their group. Flea was out next, then Ryan and Becky.

Becky had been good at a walk and better at a trot. But at a canter she was fantastic. Her technique was the same as most of the other riders. But it wasn't the way she held her reins or her seat that made her stand out. It was something about the way she communicated with Charlie. To me it seemed that Becky blocked the whole world out just the way I always had with Princess. My chest squeezed at the thought of Princess. Thinking of Princess made me think of Jenna. Thinking of Jenna made me think of my parents.

'Gary, I have to go home!' I called, running towards the gate as though I was being chased by a bunyip.

He looked at me, puzzled. 'What's wrong?'

79

'Nothing, except that I left hours ago and didn't tell Mum and Dad where I was going. They've probably got the police out looking for me by now.'

He laughed. I thought I saw Becky smile.

'By the way, I noticed your shed is a real mess.' I hadn't really. I just hoped it was. 'I do a great clean-up for only fifteen dollars.'

Gary clutched his chest. 'You'll ruin me! How does five sound?'

'Done,' I grinned as I slipped through the gate and sprinted in the direction of home.

THIRTEEN

The Fine Print

'I've circled the horses I want to look at. Can we go today?'

Dad swallowed his last spoonful of Cornflakes. 'It's the first day off I've had since we moved here. I've got unpacking to do.'

'I told you to leave it to me,' I said, spreading butter on a piece of toast. 'Only ten bucks an hour. That's dirt cheap.'

Mum took a sip of coffee. 'I thought we agreed on two dollars an hour, paid strictly on completion of the job to our satisfaction.'

'I should join a union,' I groaned, dribbling honey in circles on my toast. 'Anyway, even if it is your first day off since we moved here, what better way could you spend it than with me?'

Dad smiled over his glass of orange juice. 'How can I argue with that?'

'You can't.'

Mum looked at him sharply. I took a bite of toast. It was salty and sweet all at once.

'So can we go? They'll be sold before I've even had the chance to look at them!'

Dad made the 'time-out' gesture with his hands. 'Okay, okay. At least let me get out of my pyjamas.' He stood up and headed out of the kitchen.

Mum looked at me and sighed. 'What exactly do you have in mind for today?'

I wiped my hands on a pink paper serviette. 'Just a bit of horse-hunting. I'd really like to get my horse soon. I don't want to be folder girl at Shady Creek Riding Club forever.'

'You've only done it once. And besides, it's a great way to learn more about riding. It's very generous of Mr Cho to let you follow him around. You get to see things from the other side of the fence.'

'I still want a horse.' I stood up and began clearing

the breakfast dishes from the table. 'I'll wash up for a dollar.'

'Now you're talking affordable fees.'

'Per plate.'

Mum shook her head. 'Do it because you love your poor old mum.'

'Just this once.' I didn't want to get on her bad side, not today of all days. I was counting on this being H-Day. Horse Day.

An hour later Dad was standing in a paddock sizing up a pony who was standing placidly in his saddle and bridle. He made a grab for the classifieds. 'What did the ad say?'

'I'll read it to you,' I said. '*Dark bay nine-year-old gelding, lovely nature, ideal first pony, easy to ride and handle.*'

'They've got to be kidding,' Dad hissed.

'Shh. The owners are right over there.' I nodded my head towards a woman and a boy leaning on the fence nearby.

'I realise that, Ashleigh. But it's tiny!'

'He's all right,' I said, measuring how many of my hand-lengths went from his shoulder to the ground.

'Maybe it shrunk in the rain.'

'He's adorable!' I said, cramming the folded-up newspaper into the back pocket of my pants. 'Besides, I've always wanted a Shetland.'

Dad rolled his eyes. 'I'm not buying him for you. He only comes up to your hips.'

'But he's so sweet,' I said, rubbing the pony's tiny face. 'And he's an ideal first pony, the ad said so.'

'Ideal for a preschooler, but not for an eleven-year-old.'

'I could teach him tricks. He could wear little hats.'

'You can't ride a Shetland. Your legs would drag along the ground. Just think how silly you'd look wearing knee-pads at Riding Club,' he said, walking towards the car. 'There is no way on earth I am going to fork out my hard-earned money for a Shetland pony and that is final.'

I gave the pony a pat, smiled at the owners and climbed over the fence. Strike one. I was disappointed, but I still had two more chances.

'No way.'

'But, Dad,' I said, stroking the sleepy skewbald mare's neck. She opened one eye and peered at me briefly, then closed it again and continued to snooze.

'Ashleigh, it's old,' Dad said. 'I've never seen such an old horse. I reckon it's got a telegram from the Queen on its stable wall.'

I looked at her closely. She was about 13 hands high and had a good temperament. But Dad was right; she had to be about twenty-five. Maybe older. 'At least I'd never fall off.'

'That's true. It'd never move fast enough.'

I was starting to feel a bit anxious. Today was supposed to be H-Day and it was shaping up to be D-Day. D for Disaster. I played the only card I had.

'Dad, the Shetland I can understand. I still want to buy him for a pet, but I understand. This horse may be a bit old, but she's the perfect size for me.'

'For pity's sake, Ashleigh, it probably saw action in World War One,' Dad groaned. He looked at his watch. 'I've got unpacking to do.'

I could see that there was no way Dad would ever agree to buy the mare for me and I had to admit he was right. She was lovely, but too old to ride. I wanted a horse more than anything, but I couldn't recall a vintage horses class at any of the gymkhanas I'd competed in. I looked around for Dad. He was already in the driver's seat of the car. The engine was humming.

I rubbed the mare's velvety nose.

'Goodbye, old girl. I hope you find a nice home.' This time she didn't even wake up.

'Good things happen in threes, right, Dad?' I sent him my most hopeful expression as I unfolded the newspaper and drew a thick black cross through the ad for the sleepy old mare.

'So I hear,' he said, glancing in the rear-view mirror.

Horse number three just had to be my perfect match.

'An energetic gelding for the more adventurous rider. Perfect,' I said, grinning at the sweet-looking black horse standing in front of me. 'I'm adventurous.'

Dad scratched at his ginger beard. 'Ashleigh, I don't know about this guy. He seems a bit, um, unusual.'

'How do you mean?'

'Well, there are tons of horses in that paddock over there,' Dad said, pointing to a bunch of docile-looking ponies huddled together in a corner of the adjoining paddock. 'So why is he here?'

I stared at the corral where my horse was

standing. The fence was made of tall steel bars. It looked like a prison.

'So, can we try him out?'

'I don't know. I get the feeling he could be in solitary confinement.'

'He looks nice.' The gelding rubbed his rump against the railings.

'Well, let's see if you can catch him. That book you were torturing me with in the car said that a horse should be easy to catch. That's the first sign of a good buy.'

'Okay.' I climbed through the bars and walked over to the horse, talking to him.

'Hey, boy,' I said. 'Stand still, there's a good boy.'

I approached his near side with caution. He nodded his head and watched me from the corner of his eye.

I reached out my hand and stroked his shoulder. He quivered and stamped his foot.

'Shush,' I said, my voice smooth and sure. 'My name's Ashleigh.'

The horse flattened his ears against his head. I stopped stroking him. He bared his teeth and snapped, threatening to bite.

'Get out of there this instant!' Dad yelled.

I leapt out of the way. The horse bucked his way to the other side of the corral. He stopped suddenly and reared, rolling his eyes so that the whites showed.

I sprinted to the fence and scrambled through, Dad pulling me out by my arm. I opened my mouth, ready to plead the horse's case.

'Don't say a word, Ash. I'm not buying that horse. I wouldn't even take it for free.'

I closed my mouth and leaned against the fence staring at the horse. Now that I was out of his way, he looked as sweet natured as he had before.

I followed Dad to the car and slumped into the seat. I felt flat and miserable. H-Day had been H-Day, after all. H for Horrible.

FOURTEEN

Spiller Miller

'Why do I have to go?'

'Because you do,' Mum said.

I sighed. Mum checked her lipstick in the rear-view mirror and rubbed at a splodge of make-up under one of her eyes. She was on her way to another job interview.

It was a Monday morning. Shady Creek Primary School was open for business and I was dressed in my stiff new pale blue T-shirt and maroon shorts. They felt about as comfortable as a suit of armour. I slumped in the front seat of the car, fidgeting with the central locking button and praying for a blizzard.

'Can't I just stay home with you? Heaps of country kids do school at home on the radio.'

'I told you, Ash, I'm looking for work. If I don't work you don't eat, remember?' It was Mum's turn to sigh. 'You've already had a week off school to settle in as it is. And besides, those kids live hundreds of kilometres away from the nearest school. You, on the other hand, live only a few streets away.'

'Don't remind me.' I looked out of the window and thought about Shady Creek Primary School. What was it going to be like? Would the teacher be nice like Mr Johnson or would he be one of those crabby ones?

'Before I forget, there was an email for you last night.'

My heart jumped. There had only been one person I'd emailed since we'd moved to Shady Creek. 'From who?' I said casually.

'Jenna, I think. It was a return email.' She looked at me and raised her left eyebrow. 'Did you write to her?'

I nodded. 'A few days ago.'

'Well, I saved it to your mail folder, so when you get a chance, read it. So how do I look?' Mum sounded like someone about to go out on her first ever date.

'You look great!' I assured her, trying to sound as positive as I could, for my sake as well as hers.

'Now, have a good first day at school, possum.' She smooshed me on the cheek with her sticky red lips. 'And wish me luck!'

As I watched Mum drive away I wished I were back at my old school. With Mr Johnson and the jacaranda tree and of course, Jenna. My chest ached at the thought of Jenna. I had been avoiding even thinking about her. It just made me feel more miserable than I already was. She had made it pretty clear before I left that she and I were finished as best friends. But no matter how hard I tried to push the thought out of my head it squeezed its way back in. Shady Creek Primary would be a great place to be if only Jenna and me were here together.

'Well, look who's here.'

Dread filled me like ice-cold water. The welcoming committee was waiting. Flea, Carly Barnes and Ryan from Shady Creek Riding Club and a bunch of other kids. They were standing in a big group, looking at me as if I'd just arrived from Saturn through a gap in the clouds.

'How's your butt?' Carly sneered, her arms folded across her chest. Her hair, out of its riding school bun, was in pigtails, one at either side of her head like long, floppy bunny ears.

I summoned up all the courage I could find and swung my bag over my shoulder. 'Just fine, thanks.' I walked past them and into the playground. They followed me like baby ducks after their mum.

'Should've seen her on Scud,' Flea announced, as if I wasn't there at all. 'She went for the best spill ever.'

'What's her name?' someone else said.

I looked across the school playground at the groups of kids playing games or talking. Some of them looked at me for a moment and turned back to their friends. I walked straight ahead, not sure exactly where I was going.

'Ashleigh Miller,' said Carly. She laughed. It sounded like garbage tin lids clanging together. 'But she also answers to "Under-Twelve Champion".'

'Maybe she should start answering to Spiller,' Flea said. 'Spiller Miller! Do you get it?'

'Good one,' Ryan laughed. 'Spiller Miller.'

I stopped walking and turned around slowly. I was afraid. I knew it would be hard to start at a new school. But *this* hard?

'Why don't you just leave me alone?' I said. My voice sounded small.

'Yeah, *Frederick*.'

I looked over my shoulder. Becky Cho from Shady Creek Riding Club was standing behind me, her brown eyes flashing with rage.

Flea's mouth dropped open into a large O.

'That's his name?' I whispered.

She nodded. 'Yep. Frederick Fowler.'

Becky stared right at them, her head high, her thick black hair flowing free down her back.

'So why does he call himself Flea?' I asked, relieved that she was there.

'Could be the friends he keeps,' Becky said, regarding Flea's gang as though they were dogs that had just rolled in something very smelly. 'You know, rats.'

Carly stepped forward. 'Why don't you just be quiet, Becky?' Her ears were pink and her eyes cold.

Becky took a deep breath and stood up tall. She smiled at Carly and folded her arms. 'Who's going to make me?'

Carly and Becky watched each other, waiting to see who was going to make the first move.

Flea tapped Carly's shoulder. 'Forget it,' he said, and walked away back across the playground to the gate. His gang followed him like well-trained sheep.

Carly backed away. 'I'll get you, Spiller. And you too, Rebecca's Garden. Just you wait.' Then she was gone.

My heart pounded with relief. 'Thanks. I thought I was a goner.'

Becky smiled. 'No problem. I can't stand Flea or his dumb friends. Especially Carly.'

'Try living next door to him. I keep dreaming about dumping a truckload of horse manure through his bedroom window.'

'There's only one problem with that plan,' she said, giggling. 'He'd probably smell better. Come on, I'll show you where the office is.'

We walked off together past the handball courts and netball rings.

'So, what was all that Rebecca's Garden stuff?'

Becky rolled her eyes. 'Mum and Dad own the Chinese restaurant just over there. Dad's a chef.' She pointed past a clump of gum trees to the row of shops lined up along the main street of Shady Creek.

'You are so lucky!' I said. Becky seemed to have everything: her own horse, a horse-loving dad and an endless supply of Chinese food.

'Do you reckon? They called it Rebecca's Garden. It's so embarrassing. I wanted them to call it Trotton Inn. And besides, me and Rachael have to work there.'

'Who's Rachael?' I asked, watching a teacher set up a volleyball net.

'My sister. She goes to the High School in town. She's fifteen.'

'Does she ride as well?'

'Are you kidding? Rachael was a hot rider. Better than me and Dad. There's hardly enough room for her trophies at home any more. But she gave it all up two years ago.'

'A bad fall?'

'Nah, nothing like that.' Becky pulled a face as though she had just tasted something really yucky.

'Boys. She doesn't even look at Cassata any more, much less take care of her.'

'Cassata?'

'Rachael's horse. She's an Appaloosa. Mum and Dad couldn't bear to sell her. Neither could I. But she hardly gets ridden these days.'

Becky's face broke into a huge grin. It was the first time I'd seen her really smile.

'Ashleigh, I've got it,' she said. 'Dad told me you're looking to buy a horse of your own. How about you ride Cassata until you get one?'

'Are you for real?' I gasped.

'Of course,' Becky said, her eyes bright. 'We could ride together.'

'But will it be okay?' I asked anxiously. 'You know, with your family?'

Becky nodded. 'Mum and Dad won't mind. Cassata needs the exercise. She's nearly as big as a hippo! Oh, and this is the office.' She pointed at the old stone building in front of us.

I beamed at her, speechless for once. A horse to ride whenever I wanted and a friend to go riding with. Shady Creek was looking like the best place in the world, even with Flea living next door.

FIFTEEN

Cyberhorse

I had the whole place to myself. Mum was out making friends with Mr and Mrs Flea (you can see why I was happy to stay home alone) and Dad was doing a double shift at the hospital. It was getting late. I flopped down in the good chair, switched on the computer and stared into space, thinking while it ticked and buzzed itself into action.

Things had been funny at home lately. They hadn't said anything to me, but I could tell that my parents were worried. Dad was working more than he ever had in the city and Mum hadn't cracked a smile since the day she'd started looking for a job. Not even when I'd done my world famous monkey face that morning at breakfast. The last time I'd done it, Mum had laughed so hard coffee had come out of her nose.

The other night I'd heard her talking quietly to Dad. She'd said that she never should have left Mick's Master Plumbers. Dad hadn't said anything.

But worst of all, they kept coming up with excuses to get out of going horse-hunting with me. Just the other day I'd asked Mum to take me out to see a gelding, that sounded perfect, in Pinebark Ridge, a nearby town. She had coughed and said she had to clean all the light bulbs.

I logged on to the Net and typed *horses for sale* into the search space. Even though Becky had promised me a ride of her sister's horse, I still had to get a horse of my own. The machine made a few beeps and coughed up 1382 hits. I scrolled down and had a browse through the first ten. My shoulders drooped. They were all American sites.

I went back to the search space and typed in *Australian horses for sale*. I got 27 hits.

I scrolled down the screen again and saw *horsesonline*. I clicked on that. All the writing vanished and the screen went blue. Galloping horses appeared across the bottom and a list of names came up: *Sparky, Brandy, Grey Ghost, Teddy Bear*. I clicked on Sparky.

A photo of a palomino came up. There was writing underneath.

Sparky. Quarter horse weanling colt. Excellent conformation. Should mature to 15.2hh. Make lovely dressage horse. Quiet. By Valentio. $4000.

The foal was cute. But he was still a baby. I clicked on Brandy.

11 yo 13.2hh grey mare, loving nature, has been out of work, very green, needs confident, experienced rider. $1500.

Seeing the word 'green' made me go green. Brandy was definitely not the horse for me.

I scrolled further down the list and clicked on a horse called Jester. A picture of a bay gelding wearing a saddle and bridle came up.

Jester. 14.2hh 7 yo bay gelding, suit first horse buyer, perfect for Riding Club or pleasure. Only $550.

I liked the sound of that. I liked the look of him. I really liked the price. With the hundred and thirty-four dollars I'd saved up so far, Jester was looking like the best horse I'd seen since I moved to Shady Creek. I scribbled down the phone number.

I switched off the computer and sat next to the phone staring at the crumpled piece of paper I'd written the phone number on. I picked up the phone and dialled.

A woman answered. 'Hello.'

I cleared my throat. 'Hi, I was calling about Jester.'

'What about him?'

My heart pounded. Maybe he was already sold. Maybe the owners had changed their minds.

'Is he still for sale? I saw the ad in *horsesonline*.' I twisted the curly phone cord around my index finger as many times as it would fit.

'Oh sure, he's still for sale.'

'Great!' I said, yanking my finger free. 'I'd like to buy him.'

There was a pause at the other end of the line. 'Who am I speaking to?'

'I'm Ashleigh Miller,' I said in my most responsible voice.

'How old are you, Ashleigh Miller?'

It was my turn to pause. 'I'm eleven. But ... er ... I'll be twelve in a few months' time,' I said, hoping to sound older.'

'Do your parents know you're calling?' The voice sounded suspicious.

That was a tough one. I weighed it up in my head.

Did they know I was calling?

No.

Did they promise I could get a horse?

Yes.

'It's okay,' I said. 'My parents want me to have a horse. They said they'd buy one for me. That's why we moved to the country. And I've been saving up, too, to help them out.'

'You're sure?'

I nodded down the phone. 'Yes. I'm sure.'

'I don't know, love,' the woman said. My heart sank. But I thought fast.

'No, really, it's okay,' I said, trying to sound as convincing as an ad for laundry detergent. 'My parents know I'm calling. They said I should speak to you myself, since they don't know much about horses. And they like me to be responsible.'

Okay, so I bent the truth just a little. But it was worth it. A few minutes later Jester was mine to be floated to Shady Creek first thing the next morning and paid for, cash on delivery.

I had a horse. I finally had a horse of my own! I felt like Cinderella. A whole lifetime of dreams had come true. As I ate my dinner in front of the TV, locked all the doors and put myself to bed, I knew that nowhere in the world could there possibly be a kid as happy and lucky as me.

'Ashleigh!'

I rolled over in bed, tangled in sheets, and moaned.

'Ashleigh! Wake up this minute.'

I opened my eyes and blinked at the sunlight. Then I sat up, remembering. It was today. Jester was coming today.

I leapt out of bed and ripped open the door.

'Ashleigh Miller! Get down here this very second!'

Taking the stairs three at a time, I found my parents at the front door. They were dressed in their pyjamas and dressing gowns. Their hair was sticking up like it was in shock. Dad was pale. Mum was red.

A woman was standing outside the door dressed in boots, jodhpurs, a jumper and a jacket. A thick purple beanie with a fuzzy hot pink pompom was pulled down over her ears. She smiled warmly.

'This must be Ashleigh.'

I looked at her. Then at my parents. They glared back at me. They looked upset.

I swallowed and raised my hand a little. 'That's me.'

Purple Beanie took a step inside. I could see a sleek blue car outside with a green double horse float attached to it. I could just make out the shape of a dark horse through the window of the float. My heart bounced with excitement. I smoothed down my hair.

'I've come to deliver Jester.' She beamed at my parents. 'Ashleigh bought him yesterday evening. He's a fine horse and I'm sure they'll make a great team. I must say, I'm very impressed with your daughter. Very responsible for her age.'

Mum pulled her dressing gown tight around her and folded her arms. 'Could you give us a minute?'

The woman nodded. 'No probs. I'll just go and unload him.'

Mum closed the front door behind Purple Beanie and took a step towards me. Dad stared out of the window as Jester was backed down the ramp. He was gorgeous. I couldn't wait to cuddle him.

'Ashleigh, what have you done?' Mum hissed. She looked furious. Her face was all squashed and her eyes were like slits. Her voice sounded weird, like she was only just managing to keep it under control.

I was shocked.

'I, I,' I stammered.

I never thought they'd be mad. I thought they'd be happy that I'd taken care of it myself and not dragged them off to see another horse they might not like.

'I just thought . . . I saw this horse on the Internet and I . . .'

'Enough!' Dad snapped. 'That's it! I've had it. That horse is going right back where he came from. I can't believe it, Ashleigh. I can't believe you would do such a thing.'

I gulped. Send Jester back? 'No, Dad. Please!'

'Your father's right. This time you've gone too far. Now go upstairs and get dressed.' Mum watched me. Her eyebrows were knotted up together on the bridge of her nose. Now she looked more tired than furious.

'But—' I began.

'Now!' Mum barked. She looked like she was having some sort of fit. I'd never been so glad to have a nurse for a father.

I turned and dragged myself up the stairs. A horse, my horse, was standing in the driveway and he'd been ripped away from me before I'd even had a chance to see him face to face.

I got dressed while Dad argued with Jester's owner. I peeked out of the window. Both of them were waving their arms about. The woman didn't look so happy any more. She was shouting.

'I spent sixty bucks on petrol to transport this horse on the condition that he was sold! I want reimbursement.'

'The condition that he was sold?' Dad boomed. 'To a kid of eleven?'

My mouth went dry. I pressed my ear to the window and licked my lips as Jester was reloaded.

The woman slammed the gate of the horse float shut and secured the bolts. 'She told me it was okay. She told me you wanted her to have a horse. She said that was why you'd moved to the country!'

Dad went quiet. He disappeared inside the house and returned with a few red bills. 'Here,' he said, handing them to her. 'Your money. And I'm sorry you wasted your time.'

She folded the money into the pocket of her jacket, climbed into the driver's seat and I watched the horse float rattle down the driveway taking Jester and all my dreams away with it.

'Ashleigh, I'm going to have to punish you. That money will come out of Horse Cents,' Dad said later at breakfast, his lips thin and pale.

I sat alone at the table, staring at my breakfast. Buttered toast and raspberry jam had never been so unappetising.

'You're going to have to pay me back. Today.'

I pushed my plate away, suddenly feeling very sick. It had taken me ages to make that money and I was about to lose nearly half of it. It wasn't fair.

'Dad, please, I said I'm sorry and I meant it. I'll do anything to make it up to you, but don't take my Horse Cents money away.'

Dad shook his head. 'I'm sorry, Ash. It's the only way. You are going to have to take responsibility for your actions. Maybe you're not ready for a horse after all.'

He sat down heavily on a chair and watched me. I coughed and tried to swallow a big, dry lump. The first tears stung my eyes. Maybe Mum would help, I thought, maybe she would understand. But instead of pleading my case she was calmly spooning instant coffee granules into her favourite mug.

'Don't take my money away,' I begged.

'Your dad's right, Ashleigh. It's fair that you pay back the money. What you did was very irresponsible.'

Mum folded her arms and glanced at Dad. I put my head down on the table and sobbed. First I had lost Jester. Now I was losing half of Horse Cents.

'Ashleigh, there's something we need to tell you. Something serious,' Mum said.

I sat bolt upright, wiping my face with my hands.

'You know that I've been out of work since we moved here.'

I nodded, too upset to do anything else.

'And you know that this house cost a lot of money. What with the five acres and all.'

I nodded again.

'We had to borrow a lot from the bank and our place back home didn't sell for nearly what we expected it would.' Mum took a sip of coffee and cleared her throat. 'We're running short on money. We've done our best,' she looked at Dad again, who was scratching his beard slowly and staring at the wall, 'but I'm afraid the horse is going to have to wait.'

'What do you mean?' I said. A shiver ran down my legs.

Mum fidgeted gingerly with the handle of her mug. 'I mean we can't afford it. We're not going to be buying a horse for you. Not at the moment, anyway. I'm sorry, Ash.'

I couldn't believe what I was hearing. I shook my head, trying to take it in. I wasn't going to have a horse of my own? This couldn't be happening. It wasn't fair.

'But you promised. You said that I'd get a horse! And what about Riding Club? I can't go back there without a horse of my own.'

'I know what we said,' she said, standing up. 'But we miscalculated. Your dad and me both thought I'd just walk into a job. And I've tried to explain about the mortgage. Money doesn't grow on trees you know.'

'But I've been working so hard to make money, even though you told me I could stop!'

'Horses aren't just a one-off purchase,' Dad said. 'There's all that stuff that goes along with them. Tack, feed and vets. It never ends!'

From the sounds of it they'd been making a list.

'I don't believe you,' I yelled. 'You have the money; you just don't want me to have a horse. You never did!'

Mum's eyes widened. 'How can you say that?'

'You've never once come to see me ride.'

'That's not true,' Dad said.

'You always complained about driving me all the way to South Beach Stables,' I said hotly. 'And you've found something wrong with every single horse we've seen since we got here.'

Dad took a step towards me. 'Ashleigh, that's enough.'

I jumped to my feet. 'You promised me a horse that I'll never get. You made me move to this dump and,' I said as the tears rolled down my face, 'I gave up my best friend, for nothing.'

'Oh, Ashleigh!' Mum gasped, her eyes wide.

'I hate it here. I hate this family.'

I ran past them out of the kitchen and up the stairs to my room, slamming the door hard behind me.

SIXTEEN

Mystery Horse

'Didn't see you at Riding Club yesterday.' Becky leaned against the open door in her riding helmet, grinning at me. Her horse Charlie and her sister's horse, Cassata, were tacked up and grazing on our front lawn. Cassata was a sweet-looking Appaloosa with a dark brown face, neck and legs and a white rump covered in brown oval spots. The horses' bits jingled in their mouths as they ripped at the fresh green grass.

I shrugged. 'What's the point?' I wasn't going to be getting a horse of my own. And I didn't want to sit on the fence at Shady Creek Riding Club for the rest of my life.

Becky pushed her hands into the pockets of her pants. Her black hair was braided into two plaits, one on either side of her head. She looked like Heidi in a helmet. 'Come for a ride? Cassata's all ready to go. She's itching for a run.'

I shook my head. Since finding out the truth from my parents I'd decided to stay away from horses. It hurt too much. And knowing that all those kids from school were riding around on their own horses was like having all my broken dreams blow a huge raspberry in my face. 'Don't feel like it. Sorry, Beck.'

Becky sighed. 'Ashleigh, I went to all the trouble of catching her, tacking her up and dragging her over here. The least you could do is come for a ride. I want to show you down a new trail. And,' she pointed to a swollen saddlebag that was secured to Charlie's saddle, 'I packed some lunch.'

'Chinese food?'

'Of course.'

My stomach growled. 'Give me a minute.' I trudged upstairs for my riding hat and boots.

We rode down the driveway and around the corner past Flea's house. Flea was mucking out

Scud's corral. He looked up as we rode past, a shovel full of horse poo dangling from his hands. A poisonous grin spread across his face.

'Hang on tight, Spiller!' he yelled.

I glared at him and patted Cassata's damp neck. She was already starting to sweat.

'I want to get him so bad,' Becky moaned. 'He thinks he's so good.'

'How long has Cassata gone without exercise?' I asked. 'I shouldn't push her if she's unfit.'

Becky shrugged. 'She gets a run every week. Dad puts her on the lunge at home as well. She's still too fat, but.'

'Yeah. Fat butt, all right. So, where are you taking me?' I asked as we passed Shady Creek Riding Club. A few riders were cantering slowly around the paddock. I smiled to myself. Shady Creek was a horse-lover's paradise.

'I already told you. New trail. Goes down to the river.'

I followed Becky down a narrow dirt track that led into the bush.

Becky nudged her horse into a canter and I followed her down the track towards the river. The sunlight flickered through the trees and splashed onto our faces. The wind rushed past my ears. Whoosh! My heart raced. Cassata's hooves pounded on the dusty grey track like beating drums. I started to feel better as Becky pointed out things along the way.

'See that tree?' She pointed and called over her shoulder, her plaits flying out behind her. 'That's where a guy was bitten by a snake and dropped dead before you could say red belly. And see that track? It's haunted by the ghost of an old swagman.'

We stopped at a clearing. Becky dismounted, tethered Charlie to a tree, unbuckled her saddlebag and spread a small picnic rug on the ground. She piled plastic containers filled with food and drinks onto it and handed me an empty plastic plate. 'Load up. I'm starved.'

I pulled the lid off a container. 'What's this?'

'Ham balls. And those are spring rolls. And those little half-moon shaped ones are gow gees.'

We ate until we were as stuffed as a dim sum and lay in the sun, sleepy and warm.

'That was great,' I said, rubbing my tummy. 'Thanks.'

Becky smiled. 'No worries. Come over afterwards and I'll get Dad to make us fried ice cream.'

'Hmmm.'

'So,' Becky said, rolling over on her front and propping up her chin in her hands. 'What's happening with your horse?'

'There won't be a horse. Not yet anyway.' I told her all about Jester, my parents' big announcement and the whole petrol-money payback mess.

Becky burst out laughing. 'That's the craziest thing I've ever heard! Are you off the planet?'

I laughed with her. 'Does a horse have hooves?'

Then something that sounded like whinnying floated past on the breeze. I froze.

'What?' said Becky. 'What's wrong?'

I strained my ears for the sound. I could hear a horse whinnying. I was sure of it.

Becky sat up and our eyes locked.

'I can hear something. It's a horse.'

Becky looked around. 'Are you sure? Around here?'

I nodded and stood up. 'Positive.'

I heard it again. This time Becky heard it, too.

'You're right,' she said. 'You must have ears like a bat.'

'Let's check it out.' I helped Becky pack up our lunch things. We mounted and set off in the direction of the noise. Cassata's dark ears pricked forward. She answered the horse with a resounding whinny of her own. Charlie danced with excitement.

'What's with these two?' I stroked Cassata's brown neck.

'Horses love the company of other horses. They're looking forward to making a new friend.'

The whinnying grew louder and more frantic the deeper we rode down the track.

'It's coming from here,' I said, reaching a fence. 'We have to find a way in.'

'Let's ride along the fence.' Becky's face was flushed with excitement. 'There has to be a gate somewhere.'

The whinnying sounded again, louder than ever. Charlie nodded his head and snorted.

'There! Look!' I called.

We'd stopped in front of a gate into a property. And in the distance I could just make out a horse. Its shrill, panicked whinny sounded like an old-fashioned kettle on the boil.

'What's going on?' Becky asked, straining to see the horse properly.

'I'm not sure. But something's got to be up. Horses don't sound like that for no reason.'

I reached for the rusty chain holding the gate in place.

'We can't just go in, Ash.'

'That horse is in trouble,' I said, pushing the gate open with my foot. 'I just know it.'

Becky bit her bottom lip nervously and glanced over her shoulder. The horse whinnied again.

'Come on,' I insisted.

We rode onto the property and cantered over to investigate.

SEVENTEEN

Horse Rescue

'I can't believe it. It's disgusting.' Becky dismounted frantically and tethered Charlie to a fence post.

'Look at her!' I threw Becky my reins and rushed to the chestnut mare's side.

She was tangled in some loose wire. It was cutting into her right foreleg. She was thin, almost half the size of Cassata. Her ribs poked through her dark, honey-coloured coat. She looked at me, thirsty and miserable. My throat went all lumpy. Torn between pity and rage, all I wanted to do was cry.

I looked around the place, for any sign of her owner. There was a house on the property, but it looked empty. Dark curtains were drawn stiffly across the windows. A few shabby trees withered in the heat and only an occasional clump of dry grass poked through the hard barren earth.

'Who lives here?'

'It's a holiday house,' said Becky. 'Some rich lawyer from the city owns it. They hardly ever come here.'

'Did you know there was a horse here?'

'No way. They must have just left her here to fend for herself.' Becky's voice cracked. She was close to tears, too. 'I can't believe anyone could do this.'

I took charge. 'Becky, go get your dad. Tell him to hurry. I'll stay here with her.'

Becky nodded and scrambled into the saddle, cantering back to the fence. I ran to the house, bashing on doors and windows. But by the look of things, nobody had been home for ages.

I dashed back to the paddock in such a panic, I crashed into an old drinking trough. It was empty!

I gave it a kick. 'Empty!' I yelled. 'How could they leave a horse without water?'

I bolted around to the side of the house to the rainwater tank. A red plastic bucket hung over the tap. I filled it and carried it to the horse. Water slopped all over my boots, leaving a wet trail in the dust from the tank to the mare.

She drained the bucket and searched for more, sniffing around the bottom.

'Everything will be okay, girl,' I whispered.

She turned her head towards me and snorted. I reached my hand out towards her and touched her shoulder. I had to get a look at that cut, but she needed to trust me. I ran my hand down her leg. She stood calm and still, shifting the weight from her hurt foreleg to the other.

Her leg was a mess. The sharp wire was wrapped around it a few times. She'd tried to pull herself free, but she'd only wound up tightening it and now she couldn't move at all.

I inspected the cut. It ran straight across her fetlock. Blood had run down to her hoof and turned her white sock a rusty brown colour. It was a deep cut and I knew if the horse panicked and tried to run it would only get worse.

'There, there,' I murmured, 'we'll get you fixed up.'

I stroked her, afraid to touch her too hard. She was in a terrible condition. I could feel bones under her skin. She had cast two shoes and her hooves were overgrown. I filled with anger.

There was a crunching noise and a clank of metal. I looked up. Becky was in the front seat of her parents' car with her dad, towing a dark blue double horse float. Another car was following behind.

'Hello, Ashleigh,' Gary said as he climbed out.

I nodded tightly, patting the horse to keep her calm.

'This is our vet, Amanda Filano. I was lucky enough to catch her on her way out to Pinebark Ridge. From what Becky's told me, we might need her.'

A young woman dressed in a white T-shirt and black pants smiled at me and extended her hand. I shook it, relief rushing through me like cool water.

'Hi,' I said, stroking the mare's chestnut neck.

'She's not looking too good, is she?' Amanda said, opening her bag.

'Who would do a thing like this?' I raged. 'There's nobody home. She's starving. The water in that old trough has dried up. Did they seriously think she could turn on the tap all by herself?'

Amanda ran her hands down the mare's neck and along her back, then looked carefully at her legs.

'I'll give her a thorough examination in a moment. The first thing we have to do is get her out of this wire.'

Gary stepped forward, clipped the wire with wire cutters and removed it slowly from the mare's leg.

'It's fresh,' he said. 'She's lucky you girls found her when you did.'

Amanda pressed a clean gauze pad on the cut and smiled at me. 'Here, hold this for me.'

I held it in place until Amanda cleaned the cut with some antiseptic and clipped away the hair around it. She cleaned it again and pulled a needle out of her bag.

'What's that for?' I asked. I hate needles.

'If you're squeamish, don't look.'

I held tight to the horse's shabby rope halter and concentrated on looking over her shoulder while her leg was sutured and a pressure bandage was wrapped around the cut to hold the stitches in place.

'All done.' Amanda dug around in her bag again and pulled out another needle.

'Not again,' I moaned.

'It's a tetanus shot. Comes with the territory, I'm afraid.' Amanda stood up and rubbed the horse's shoulder for a few moments before giving her the shot.

Then Amanda looked into my eyes. Her face was solemn. 'I have to be honest with you, Ashleigh,' she said. 'She's in very poor condition. Aside from the wound and quite serious malnutrition, she's probably full of worms, her eyes are a mess, and she's got greasy heel on her right hind leg.'

I looked from her to Gary and Becky. 'What are you saying?'

'The eyes and heel are easy enough to take care of and I'll give her a worm paste in a minute. But her condition . . .' Amanda sighed. She ran her hand gently over the mare's ribs. 'To be frank, if she doesn't get proper care, I may have to consider putting her down.'

I looked around at the others again. Becky was crying softly into a tissue.

'No, you can't!' I shouted.

'You don't seem to understand,' Amanda said. 'Horses this sick usually don't make it without time, money and care to bring them back to condition. And I really think time has run out for her.'

'That's not fair!' I said, tightening my grip on her headstall. 'You're not even giving her a chance.'

Amanda gave the mare a pat and motioned to Gary. They walked away together and stood in front of the Chos' car, whispering.

I rubbed the mare's forelock, fighting back hot tears. I knew I had to fight for her. She wasn't mine, but I felt connected to her in the same way I'd been to Princess. And besides, by the sound of Amanda Filano, if I didn't try to save the mare, nobody would.

I watched Becky lead Cassata up the ramp of the horse float. Then it hit me. An idea so hugely amazing it burst out of me like a volcano. 'Please, let me have her. I'll look after her!'

Amanda stopped whispering and looked at Gary, raising her eyebrows.

'I really should take her with me,' she said. 'I'll need to contact the RSPCA.'

'I can look after her,' I begged.

'I'll have to speak to your parents first. And I'd like to see your backyard as well to make sure it's suitable for a horse of her size.'

'Backyard?' Becky cried. 'They've got five acres!'

'That's right!' I gushed. 'And a stable and a barn. And my parents won't mind at all.'

'I don't know,' Amanda said, glancing at Gary.

Gary shrugged as if to say 'up to you'.

'Please! At least just ask Mum and Dad. They'll say yes, I know they will.'

'And this way she'll get all the care she needs,' Becky said, smiling at me. 'Ash loves horses more than anyone I know.'

'Well,' said Amanda, smiling. 'Let's get her into the float, then.'

EIGHTEEN

Home is Where the Horse Is

'You must be kidding,' Dad said, poking the mare's side.

'It's a broken-down bag of bones.' Mum looked like she'd just seen a UFO or something.

'A broken-down fleabag of bones,' Dad added. 'It looks like a xylophone. I could play "Baa Baa Black Sheep" on its ribs.'

This wasn't the reaction I'd hoped for. I ran my hand down the mare's neck and tried to swallow the hurt and anger that was rising up in my chest. This was a horse they were talking about. Sometimes I got the feeling they just didn't understand me at all. 'She's not an it, she's a she.'

'We're sorry, possum,' Mum said, touching my hair. 'It's just that she looks so sick.'

'But I want her. I want to look after her.' I swallowed again. There was something huge and sticky in my throat like a huge slurp of cold, lumpy porridge that was just refusing to go down.

'Come off it, Ash,' Dad moaned, looking at the sky like he hoped to find all the answers written across it.

'She's not worth it,' Mum said. 'You'll put all this love and attention into her and it won't be enough to bring her back to condition.'

'Just let the vet take her,' Dad murmured, giving my hand a squeeze, 'and hand her over to the RSPCA.'

'You wouldn't say that about one of your patients,' I muttered. I had expected Dad, of all people, to understand.

Dad frowned. 'Ashleigh! That's enough. People are people. But this is a horse.'

'Does that mean she's not worth saving?' I cried.

Mum and Dad exchanged weary glances and sighed.

I snuck a peek at Amanda who was talking on her mobile phone. To send the mare away with Amanda would mean only one thing. Didn't my parents get it?

'We said we'd get you a horse and we meant it,' Mum said at last. 'But not now. Wait a while.'

'But why?' I whined. 'Look at her. She needs me. And I need her.'

'Why you?' Dad asked, patting the mare's shoulder. 'Why this horse?'

I shrugged and held on tight to the mare's halter. She rubbed her face on my shoulder. I had to have her, no matter what. If my parents didn't understand that, she was doomed.

'I'll take good care of her,' I promised. 'I'll spend every cent I've got to make her better, and I'll work hard at extra jobs, too.'

They looked at one another again. Mum shrugged. Dad raised his eyebrows.

'Come on, Mum,' I begged. 'She won't cost you anything.'

'Up to you, Helen,' Dad said. He always says that when he doesn't want to make a decision.

'It's just not a good time,' she said.

'But, *Mum*. They're going to put her down. They'll,' I strained to say the terrible word, '*kill* her!' I looked up at her with pleading eyes.

'I can't believe I'm agreeing to this but, I suppose it's all right,' she said at last, throwing up her hands in what I could only assume was thanks to the horse gods.

'But you've got to take good care of her.' Dad folded his arms across his chest. 'And you have to do well at school.'

'And keep your room in a state fit for human habitation,' Mum added. She must have known I'd agree to anything.

'And remember,' Dad said. 'She already has other owners. She's just here for a little while. So don't get too attached to her, okay?'

That was true, but what did I care? The owners were kilometres, ages, worlds away from Shady Creek. And they seemed to have forgotten all about the chestnut mare.

I rushed over and threw my arms around Mum and Dad, squeezing tight.

'Have I ever let you down?'

Strangely, they didn't answer.

'And I've thought up a great name for her,' I gushed. 'I'm going to call her Honey!'

NINETEEN

Touch and Go

'C'mon, Honey, eat!' I held a bucket of bran mash under my new friend's nose. She stood before me with her head hung low, barely aware that I was even there.

'Honey, please. You must eat something.' I felt desperate. Honey ignored me and closed her eyes. Her knees crumpled suddenly and she stretched out flat on the grass. I bit hard at my bottom lip and scooped a handful of mash from the bucket.

Crouching next to Honey, I held the gooey mixture under her nose. Her bottom lip fell open but her eyes remained shut.

'Eat,' I pleaded. 'You'll never get well if you keep this up.'

For a moment I considered shoving it down her throat, but I knew it was pointless. She just wasn't interested in eating.

It had been going on for days. Since Becky and I had rescued Honey she'd been getting worse. She was spending most of her time asleep and had refused to eat anything. She'd hardly had anything to drink either. I was so worried. Amanda Filano was dropping in today and I knew exactly what she'd say when she saw that Honey had made no progress.

I ran my hand over the mare's ribs, feeling each one hard under my fingers. Her hips stuck out like wings. Dad had even joked that he could hang a hat on them to try to cheer me up. Needless to say, it hadn't worked.

'How's it going?'

I squinted over my shoulder. Becky, mounted on Charlie, was looking as worried as I felt. In comparison to Honey, super-fit Charlie looked positively obese.

'No good,' I sighed. 'As you can see.'

'Has she eaten anything?' she asked, slipping down from Charlie's back.

I shook my head.

'I got your homework for you.' Becky unzipped her school bag and pulled out a few sheets of paper. 'How much longer are you going to be away?'

I shrugged. It made me sick to think of what could happen to Honey if I left her alone for a whole six hours. 'I can't leave her alone like this all day.'

Becky smiled despite herself as she loosened Charlie's girth. 'I still can't believe your parents have let you take time off school to look after her. That only happens in the movies.'

'Nobody's more freaked than me. It was their idea, too.'

When Mum had first suggested a few days away from school to take care of Honey I had suggested a visit to the doctor. It would have been a dream come true except Honey seemed to have been better off without me. And the fact I'd overheard Dad telling Mum that the wreck of a nag in the paddock had better get better before the vet bill went through the roof made me want to smash something.

I chewed on my thumbnail and looked at my watch. Amanda was due any minute. I laid my hands on Honey's head, willing her to get better right away. We'd only been together a little while, but I didn't know what I would do without her. I didn't even want to think about it.

'I want the truth, Ashleigh. How long has she been like this?' Amanda Filano looked into Honey's eyes, frowning.

I rubbed my forehead. 'Since the day after we found her. She was okay that night. She grazed and had some water. But the next morning ...'

'Yes?' she prompted, looking severe.

I sighed. 'She was like this.'

Amanda breathed out hard through her nose, glaring at me. She was furious. I stared at the grass, scared. I hated being in trouble.

'You should have called me straight away. How could you be so irresponsible?'

My throat tightened. Why was 'irresponsible' everyone's favourite Ashleigh-adjective lately? And besides, I'd been looking after Honey all day and practically all night for days. I'd missed school, hardly slept, forgotten to eat and I was worried out of my mind! But my biggest fear of all was that Amanda would take one look at Honey and decide to put her down. I just needed more time.

'I thought I could handle it.'

'Well you were wrong!' Amanda snapped, ripping open her black leather vet bag. 'If I'd known this was going to happen I would never have left her here.'

I burst into tears. Becky put her arm around me and patted my back. 'She's tried, Amanda. She really has.'

Amanda's face softened slightly, but she was still upset. 'First I have to examine Honey. Then I'm going to decide whether or not to take her with me. She needs to be cared for properly by someone who knows what they're doing.'

I nodded, sniffling, and rubbed my runny nose on my sleeve.

Amanda laughed. 'Nice manners.'

She poked at Honey for a while and eventually managed to get her up on her shaky legs. I held Honey's headstall, but there was really no need; Honey wasn't in a rush to go anywhere.

'I don't know,' Amanda said at last. 'I just don't know what could be bothering her. Maybe I should worm her again.'

'Do you think that'll make a difference?' I asked, hope burning in my chest for the first time in days.

Amanda rifled through her bag. 'It's worth a shot. The first paste should have worked but she may have spat it out, I suppose. We were so distracted. I don't have a stomach drench with me, we'll just have to try a paste again.'

She pulled out a worming paste syringe and a measuring tape. She measured Honey's middle with the tape and dialled her weight on the syringe. 'Hold Honey tight for me, will you? She's not a big fan of worming paste.'

I clung to Honey's headstall and stroked her neck.

Amanda pushed the syringe back into Honey's mouth and depressed the plunger, squirting the paste down her throat.

'Will she get better?' I asked, patting Honey's shoulder.

'I'm afraid I don't know.' Amanda loaded everything back into her vet bag.

'If it's just a case of worms, she'll get better and I can keep her, right?' I tangled my fingers in Honey's golden mane, praying that Amanda would say yes.

Amanda shrugged. 'It will depend on how much of this paste goes down. Some horses can be sneaky and spit it out when you're not looking. I think Honey may be one of those. She might need that drench after all. So we'll just have to see.'

I sighed, relieved. A 'we'll see' was better than a 'no'.

'If she picks up over the next day or so, and that's a big if, I'll consider letting her stay on here.'

'Yes!' I shouted. Becky and I high-fived.

'But,' Amanda said, shaking her hair out of her eyes, 'if there is no improvement in her condition after the drench, I will have no other choice but to take her away and find her some expert care.'

I nodded. 'Okay.' What else could I say?

'One more thing,' Amanda added gently. 'If she continues to get worse, I'll have to put her down. It's the only humane thing to do. Do you understand?'

'No!' I shouted, all the emotions of the last few days bursting out. 'I don't. Looking after her is the only humane thing to do. Helping her to get better. Isn't that a vet's job?'

Amanda's eyes narrowed and she sucked in her breath. 'I'd advise you not to use that tone with me. Do you understand that?'

I flushed, hanging my head, and feeling ashamed of myself. 'Yes.'

Amanda slipped through the fence and stalked off to her car. Becky grabbed my arm.

'She's a top vet, Ash. I can't believe how rude you were.'

Neither could I. I knew I'd be grounded until I qualified for the pension if Mum and Dad found out. But I wanted to fight for Honey. And I knew I had to do whatever it took.

TWENTY

Last Chance

I poked at my taco. There was no way I could eat it, although tacos were one of my favourites and I knew Dad had made them just for me.

But eating was the last thing on my mind. I was so worried about Honey. She'd shown no improvement at all. She'd refused every scrap of food I'd offered her, from the bran mash to sugar lumps, and had only taken a few small sips of water from a bucket. I didn't know what to do any more. Maybe Amanda was right. Maybe she needed an expert's care.

'What's up?' Dad asked, biting into a crunchy taco. Red meat sauce spurted out either side, huge chunks of lettuce raining down on his plate. He could usually polish off a taco in two bites. Once he'd even shoved one into his mouth whole.

I pushed my plate away. His table manners were enough to turn anyone off their food, with or without horse stress. 'Nothing.'

Dad smiled through a mouthful and took a long drink from a glass of water. 'These are really hot. I think two packets of taco powder were two too many. The chillies probably didn't help either.'

I took my plate to the bin and scraped in my uneaten dinner.

'We need to get some chooks,' Mum said. 'I hate wasting good food.'

'One peck at those tacos and the eggs would be smoking!' Dad laughed at his own dumb joke.

Mum watched as I rinsed my plate and stacked it on the counter. 'What's this all about, Missy? You can only be after cash. You never do chores for free any more.'

'The expenses never stop with horses,' I said, filling the sink with hot water. I added two squirts of dishwashing liquid and swirled it all around with my fingers until frothy white bubbles bloomed. 'You said so yourself.'

I piled the dishes into the sink and scrubbed at them with a sponge, trying not to think about Honey. Every time I looked at her or thought about her, Amanda's words smashed back into my head. *If she continues to get worse, I'll have to put her down. It's the only humane thing to do.*

I felt a hand on my shoulder.

'Is anything wrong, Ash?' Mum murmured.

I nodded and scrubbed hard at a crack on one of the plates.

'It's Honey, isn't it?'

I nodded again. Everything went blurry, like I was peering through a car windscreen in a rainstorm.

'Call the vet.'

I let the plate I was torturing slip under the water and twisted around. 'I can't.'

Mum frowned. 'Why not?'

Why not? Only a hundred reasons. Amanda could take her from me or decide to shoot her on the spot. I couldn't afford to pay her for another visit just yet anyway. I'd been so busy over the last week I hadn't done a single odd job. And after the Jester fiasco and all the uneaten feed I'd bought for Honey, Horse Cents was totally bankrupt. Besides, more than anything, I needed to prove I could look after Honey myself.

'But it's late. It's already dark.'

'Just call her,' Mum urged.

'I haven't got the money!' I cried.

Mum rolled her eyes. 'We'll cover this one. Right, Grant?'

Dad choked on his third taco. Mum took it as a 'yes'.

'But why?' I said, confused. 'I thought you wanted nothing to do with it.'

'I can't stand it any more!' Mum wailed. 'You've been moping around with a face like a wet week for too long. If getting the vet out means Honey getting better and getting you happy again, it's worth every cent! But just this once.'

I smiled cautiously. 'Are you sure?'

Mum nodded. Her eyes were serious. 'Honey's looking worse than ever. I don't think you can wait any longer.'

'Ashleigh, this is Honey's last chance.'

Amanda fidgeted with a long tube and shook up a bottle of something.

I kissed Honey's nose and patted her neck. 'What is it?'

'It's the drench. It should kill anything that the pastes didn't. And it's pretty obvious she didn't get a full dose. Hold that torch for me, will you?'

I shone the torch on Honey's nose but turned away while Amanda pushed the tube into her stomach. Honey didn't even flinch. She was too weak. In a few moments it was over and Amanda pulled the tube back out.

'I just don't understand,' I said, slapping at the mosquitoes that were banqueting on my legs. 'How could worms be making Honey so sick?'

Amanda packed up her bag. 'All horses have them. But when a horse is weak or ill, or very young or old, they have less resistance. Sometimes they can even die. Our girl here just wasn't strong enough.'

As if on cue, Honey's knees gave way and she collapsed on the ground. Amanda ripped open her bag again and pulled out a stethoscope. 'She's okay,' Amanda said at last. 'Just exhausted.'

I sat down next to Honey and stroked her face, hoping, praying that she'd get better.

'Coming inside?'

I shook my head. 'I want to stay with her.'

Amanda stretched out her hand. 'Come on. You'll be carried off by the mozzies in a minute.'

'Just for a little while,' I promised.

'Suit yourself. But don't annoy her, okay?'

'Okay,' I said. 'And Amanda?'

'Yep?'

I cleared my throat and chewed on my thumbnail. 'I, um, I'm . . . I'm sorry I was so rude to you yesterday.'

Amanda folded her arms and raised her eyebrows.

'I was just so worried about Honey and sometimes I, um, I . . .'

'Yes?'

I appealed to the moon to get me out of it. It had nothing to say.

'I open my mouth before I think.'

Amanda smiled. 'You can say that again!'

We laughed. I knew I was forgiven.

Amanda climbed through the rails of the fence and crunched up to the house where a hot cup of coffee and a slice of Mum's orange cake were waiting for her. Once she was inside, I sat down next to Honey in the grass. Her eyes were half-closed and her breathing was heavy and slow. She was so tired. It was like she'd given up. She'd finally found someone to love her and she'd just given up. It seemed like she almost wanted to die.

I ran my hands over her beautiful golden face.

'Please,' I whispered. 'Please get better. I can't lose you. I already lost Jenna. I can't lose you too.'

Honey's eyes fell shut.

'Honey, listen to me. You have to live. I need you.'

I leaned over her, whispering in her ear. 'I'll always look after you. You'll never go back there, I promise.'

The back door opened. I could see Mum's familiar outline in the open doorway.

'Ashleigh!' she called. 'Come inside now and leave the poor creature in peace.'

The door closed again. I just had one more thing to say. I wanted Honey to hear it just in case.

I stroked her soft velvety ear and whispered again. 'I love you.'

Her eye flickered open for a second and shut again.

I got up and ran inside.

TWENTY-ONE

Florence Martingale

'I can't believe it's the same horse.' Becky stared at Honey in astonishment. 'When did Amanda do the drench?'

'A week ago, remember?' I said.

'It's only been two days since I last saw her, but she seems so much better!' Becky shook her head, amazed.

'If she didn't have the drench, she'd probably have died.' I shuddered at the thought. I didn't want to ever go through that again.

I leaned on the fence, watching Honey graze. Since the drench she'd improved so much. She was eating, drinking and spending much more time on her feet. She had a long way to go before she looked like dressage pony material, but she was alert and seemed to be out of danger. Honey drank deeply from her newly installed trough and walked away.

'What's this?' I asked, gesturing at the brown cardboard box Becky was carrying. *Fresh Juicy Apples* was written down one side in fat red letters.

'A present for you,' she said, grinning. She was wearing her blue Shady Creek Riding Club cap. 'For Honey, actually.'

She thrust it into my arms. Apples were a nice thought, but it wasn't something either Honey or I desperately needed. What we needed was more feed and money to pay for Amanda's next visit.

'Thanks.'

I opened the lid of the box. The familiar smell of horses wafted upwards.

'They're a bit scungy, but chuck 'em in a bucket of warm soapy water and they'll be as good as new.'

The box was packed to the brim with brushes for Honey. There were purple and red dandy-brushes with black and white bristles, black rubber currycombs, sweat scrapers with long handles, huge rectangular sponges, a shiny silver hoof pick and a few bottles of yellow horse shampoo.

I was amazed. 'Thanks, Beck, thanks a lot. She'll be the best-looking horse around.'

'We've got stacks of gear at home. Just wash them and rinse them really well with clean water. Actually,' Becky looked around over her shoulder, 'let's do it now. We can put them out to dry in the sun.'

We walked to the hose out the back. I smiled to myself. Becky was definitely the best friend I had in Shady Creek. Aside from the time we spent together at school, Becky came to see me and Honey most afternoons, just the way it had been with me and Jenna, and had even missed a precious day at Riding Club to help. My stomach flip-flopped. I missed Jenna so much. She'd only emailed once and it had been short. Just a hello and to say she was fine. As usual, I tried to push her out of my mind, but she snuck back in anyway, smiling her trademark smile, her blue eyes twinkling.

Becky put the box down and unravelled the hose while I dug around in the laundry for a bucket and some soap powder. 'What's happening with Honey's owners?'

'I don't know,' I replied. 'Amanda said she's going to deal with it.'

Becky glanced at me, her dark eyes serious. 'What if they want her back?'

I shook soap into the bucket. 'I don't care. They're not getting her back. They don't deserve her!'

Becky nodded and switched on the hose. Water sprayed into the bucket. It filled with soapy white suds. 'Anyway, I'd better go.'

'Okay, thanks for the stuff.'

'No problem,' she said, heading off.

I laid out all the brushes, now clean and brand-new looking, in neat rows on the back steps and grabbed the crate-load of medicines and creams and a few essential grooming items for Honey that I'd collected in the last few days. I shoved a few carrots and the hoof pick into my pockets and headed off into the back paddock.

'How's it goin', Spiller?' Flea shrieked over the fence from next door. 'Nice looking bag of dog meat ya got back there!' He cackled like the wicked witch of Shady Creek as he groomed his horse, Scud.

I ignored him, which I thought was pretty cool of me, finally finding Honey underneath a tree way down by the back fence. She whinnied and nodded her head when she saw me.

'What are you doing hiding down here?' I said, panting.

She snorted in response.

'Got a treat for you, girl,' I approached her, pulling a carrot out of my pocket. She craned her neck forward, stepped towards me, took the carrot and crunched it happily. I offered her another carrot and approached her near side, patting her shoulder. She felt better under my hand. Softer. There seemed to be more of her there already. I ran my hand along her back and down each of her legs, checking carefully for any cuts, lumps or botfly eggs. I also needed to clean her feet.

I picked up her hoof and held it carefully, pulling the hoof pick out of my back pocket. I cleaned out her hoof from her heel to her toe, chatting to her about my day while I worked. She was a good listener.

'She's looking well.'

I spun around. Honey's ears pricked forward. Dad smiled at me from under the tree he was leaning against.

'How long have you been there?' I said, pushing my hair out of my eyes.

'A while.' He walked over and stood next to Honey, patting her a few times. He smiled at her. 'You know, I'm really impressed.'

'About what?' I said, standing up to look in Honey's eyes. They had been a little weepy when Becky and I had found her, but the bathes with lukewarm water had cleared them up nicely.

'About the way you're taking care of Honey. It's really great. I never expected that you'd be so dedicated. And you're working so hard to pay for her, too.'

I stared at him, confused. 'Why wouldn't I?'

He shrugged. 'I don't know. I guess I thought, and Mum thought, that all this horse stuff was a phase you'd grow out of. That a few days of round-the-clock care and paying for vets would cure you once and for all.'

I stared at him with eyes as round as rice crackers. 'Me! Grow out of horses?' I laid the palm of my hand across his forehead as though he had a fever. 'Are you feeling all right?'

'Okay, okay,' he laughed.

I turned my attention back to Honey and selected a yellow body brush with soft black bristles from my crate to give her a gentle groom. She rubbed her nose against my shoulder and nibbled on my shirt.

'Anyway,' he said, brushing a fly from his nose, 'I'll leave you to it.'

I waved at him. 'See ya.'

'See you too, Florence.'

I put my hands on my hips and watched him walk away. 'Who?'

'Florence Nightingale,' he called over his shoulder. 'Only the world's most famous nurse!'

'Make that Florence Martingale!'

Dad screwed up his face. 'Martingale?'

'A martingale is a piece of tack that stops a horse from throwing its head up.' I sighed, killing off any hopes I may have had of a career in comedy. At least Becky would have got it.

It was his turn to put his hands on his hips. 'So who's Florence Martingale, then?'

I smiled. 'Only the world's most famous horse nurse!'

TWENTY-TWO

Rearing to Go

'She's doing really well. Good on you, Ash!' Amanda Filano opened the gate into our corral.

I nodded and rubbed under Honey's forelock. That always made her sleepy and relaxed.

Amanda was right. Honey was looking fantastic. I almost couldn't believe it myself. Only a few weeks ago I thought I would lose her, but now . . .

Honey nuzzled my other hand with her silky white muzzle, looking for a carrot or a slice of apple.

'I've been handfeeding her lucerne chaff every day. She gets linseed meal mixed every second day and horse pellets twice a week. Just like you said.'

Amanda seemed pleased. 'That's good. It's important that she gets an increasing plane of nutrition week by week in terms of volume and quantity.'

'Huh?'

She laughed and opened up her black leather vet bag. 'That means you have to increase what she eats slowly, which is what you're doing.'

'Good,' I said, feeling pleased with myself.

'She'll need one more shot of antibiotics, just to be on the safe side.'

I clung to Honey's headstall and stroked her neck while Amanda jabbed, poked and prodded. Honey jerked her head back in protest a few times, making me wince in sympathy.

'It's a shame, you know,' said Amanda, patting Honey's neck.

'What is?' I gave Honey's forelock an extra good rub.

Amanda packed everything away into her bag and zipped it up. 'Your Honey used to be quite a champion. Won all the local events. Won at State level too, a few times.'

'In what?'

'Jumping, novelty, gymkhanas. She was a top horse.'

'How do you know?'

Amanda swung her bag onto her back and headed for the gate. 'I thought she looked familiar the day you found her, so I did a little digging.'

'So what's her real name?'

'Argonaut.'

I grimaced. 'That's horrible. Honey is a much nicer name.'

'I agree,' Amanda said, nodding. 'She still could be a champion, you know, with time and effort. She won't win straight away. But give her a year to be back to her old condition and I think she'll show you a thing or two.'

I opened the gate and let Amanda through. 'Thanks. I reckon she will, too.'

'I'll see you again in a month.'

'Okay.' I swung the gate closed. I was disappointed that she hadn't given me the all clear to go riding. But if Honey needed more time, I could wait.

Amanda stopped and turned to me. 'Oh, you can start light rides, just locally.'

'Yes!' I jumped up and down.

'But no galloping,' she said sternly. 'And definitely no sporty stuff. Just take it slowly. She needs time to get back into it.'

I saluted her. 'Yes, ma'am!'

'And one more thing. I got a call yesterday. About Honey's owners.'

My mouth went dry. I had been hoping that if I forgot about them they would go away. 'What did they want?'

'To talk about Honey's future. Here's their number.'

'Oh.'

Amanda pulled a crumpled yellow note out of her pocket and pressed it into my hand. 'They want you to ring them. Okay?'

I nodded, feeling as though I'd just been trampled by a herd of zebras. Ring Honey's owners? They were the last people on the planet I wanted to talk to. They could take Honey away from me. They could let her stay. The choice was theirs.

Amanda looked at the ground for a moment and scuffed at a patch of dirt with her boot. 'Now, about the bill.'

I gulped. I had been dreading this almost as much as the news from Honey's owners.

Mum was getting work every few days now, and she'd made good her promise to pay for the drench. But Dad had been working so many extra shifts I hardly ever saw him any more. With that, and the shock waves of the Jester incident still rippling through the Miller household, I didn't want to ask my parents for money. Horse Cents was just managing to break even with the odd jobs I had been able to start doing around Shady Creek. But feed, vets and farriers cost a whole lot more than I'd ever thought they would.

'I can give you thirty-four dollars now as a deposit,' I said. 'It's all I've got left. But I'm working on it.'

That was true. Gary had promised me ten dollars to clean all the Cho family's saddles and Becky said she'd help.

Amanda smiled and accepted the money. 'I usually give people two weeks to pay. But you're going to have to be an exception. Just pay me when you can.'

I sighed with relief, but I knew I had to think fast. I needed to come up with some winning ideas for Horse Cents now more than ever.

TWENTY-THREE
Honey, I'm Home!

'You may as well get it over with. Save yourself the agony of not knowing.' Becky fidgeted with the note that Amanda had written the phone number on a whole week ago.

I shook my head and rocked back and forth in my chair. 'I can't. I just can't.'

I stood up and walked to the window. Honey was grazing in the paddock right opposite. All my hard work had paid off. Her coat was sleek and shiny, her heel had cleared up, her cut had all but disappeared and her eyes were bright and healthy. Only she wasn't mine yet. Amanda had made a few calls to her owners. She had threatened them with legal action.

Now they wanted me to call them, but I didn't know what to say. They had the power to take Honey away from me or to let her stay. And from our very first ride around the paddock, I knew we were meant to be together always.

Becky stood next to me and slipped her arm around my back. 'Just call. And if you need me, I'll be here.'

I nodded and sat down, squeezing the receiver nervously. My stomach jumped about like there was a team of ping-pong players warming up for a big match inside it. I stared at the number on the page and dialled with shaky fingers.

The phone rang a few times.

'They're not home,' I said, relieved. 'I'll call later.'

Just as I was about to slam the phone down, someone at the other end picked up.

'Hello,' said a man.

I stared at Becky, feeling helpless. She made huge talking mouth movements with her fingers.

'Hello, who's there?' the voice said down the line.

'Um, I ... my name is Ashleigh. Ashleigh Miller from Shady Creek.' Becky flexed her muscles superhero-style. 'I wanted to speak to someone about Honey.'

'Oh, you mean Argonaut.'

'Yes. Well, no. I call her Honey.'

The man at the other end was silent for a moment. 'Well, we call her Argonaut. But for the sake of getting this over and done with, let's just refer to her as "the horse".'

I didn't like the sound of that. But the man didn't sound like someone who liked to be argued with.

'Go on then,' he snapped. 'What do you want?'

I swallowed and clung to the phone. This man was so rude. I couldn't believe it. He gave Flea a run for his money.

'I ... er ... um ... I ...' I was so nervous, I could barely speak.

'Out with it, kid!'

I swallowed again and tried to think of calming things, like foals playing in the grass, and how Honey looked with the morning sunlight shining on her coat.

'I was hoping you'd let me keep the horse.'

There was laughter on the other end of the phone. 'Why?'

160

'Because you left her all alone to starve to death. I rescued her.'

'I've had a few calls from some vet from Shady Creek,' he went on. 'She too seems to think she has a case against me for neglect. However she also tells me that you trespassed onto my property and kidnapped my horse. Now who's got the case?'

'But, Mr ... um,' I stammered, feeling sweat soak my palms.

'Harrison.'

'Mr Harrison. If me and my friend Becky hadn't found Hon, I mean, *the horse* when we did, she might be dead by now!'

Becky bounced in her chair, applauding.

'That's beside the point,' he snapped. 'You stole my horse from my private property and now you expect me to let you keep her. That's outrageous!'

'But,' I said, feeling more helpless than I ever had in my life, 'but I've worked so hard and she's doing so well! Can't you just think about it?'

'I have thought about it, and it's just lucky for you that I've put the Shady Creek property on the market or I'd be there on your doorstep to deal with you personally.'

'You put the property on the market?'

'Yes.'

'So,' I said slowly, 'What's going to happen to the horse?'

Becky stood up and held out her hand, her eyebrows knotted together.

I gave her the phone.

'Please,' she begged. 'Let Ash keep Honey. She's doing so well. They were made for one another. If you could see them together you'd understand.'

I beamed at Becky. She smiled and handed the phone back, then played an imaginary violin.

I pressed the phone against my ear. The other end of the line was silent. Had he hung up? Or had Becky's speech moved him to guilt-ridden tears?

'Hel ... hello?' I stammered.

'Yes, I'm still here,' Mr Harrison said. 'Dabbing at my eyes.'

'Good,' I sighed.

'If your friend is done trying to tug at my heartstrings I'd like to finish this once and for all.'

I gulped and crossed my fingers. Becky crossed hers as well.

'It won't do me any good keeping the useless old

fleabag now that I'm selling up that dustbowl,' he said. 'Not to mention the fact I could do without some hick animal doctor breathing down my neck.'

I bristled. How could he say such things about Amanda when she'd done so much to save Honey? But I tried to stay calm.

'What are you saying?'

Becky jabbed the speaker button on the phone so that she could hear the news. Mr Harrison's voice flooded into the room.

'Keep her. I've got no use for her now.'

I grinned and threw my arms around Becky's neck. We danced around the room together, crashing into the furniture.

'Thank you!' I yelled into the phone.

'But I never want to hear from you again, kid. Understand?'

'Yes!' I shrieked. 'You can count on it.'

'And tell that vet to get off my back, do you read me?'

'Loud and clear,' I sang.

Mr Harrison slammed down the phone and it was over.

Honey was mine forever.

That night after dinner at Becky's restaurant, I logged on to the Net and opened my mail folder.

It was empty.

I clicked on *New Message*, typed in an address and began to write.

Hi Jenna,

I have some news I just had to tell you.

It's finally happened. I got my horse!

Her name is Honey and she's chestnut and so beautiful and I love her more than anything in the world. You have to come and see her!

The vet says I can ride her now (she was a bit sick when I first got her). And I'm going to join Shady Creek Riding Club and go on camps and to rallies and meets and it's going to be unreal.

How's everything in the city?

Love from Ash and Honey.

PS. I miss you heaps. Write back to me soon.

TWENTY-FOUR
A Real Chestnut

'Would anyone care to know who the Teams Events teams for this year's Shady Creek and Districts Annual Zone Gymkhana are?' The members of Shady Creek Riding Club sat mounted on their horses, staring at Gary Cho. I was dazed. It had only been ten weeks since Honey had become my horse, and here we were, fully-fledged members of Shady Creek Riding Club.

'I certainly would,' Carly said, smoothing down her tie. There were murmurs of agreement from the rest of the club.

'Okay,' Gary continued. 'The Under-Twelves team is Carly Barnes on Destiny.'

Becky and I applauded, rolling our eyes.

'Becky Cho on Charlie.'

'As if there was any doubt,' Carly said, her eyes narrowing with disgust.

'Flea Fowler on Scud.'

Ryan and Flea high-fived each other. I glanced at Becky. One more spot. It was between me and Ryan. We crossed our fingers.

'And finally, Ashleigh Miller on Honey.'

'Yes!' Becky shrieked. I let out a huge sigh of relief. This was what I wanted to hear. Not even joining the club in the first place meant as much to me as being on *that* team. I needed to show Flea, Carly, Ryan and everybody else at Shady Creek Riding Club I was just as good as they were. And that Honey was the most brilliant horse around. My head was spinning. It was my dream come true.

Gary read out the names of the other teams and folded up his piece of paper.

Ryan looked confused. 'But what about me? What team am I going to be in?'

Gary frowned. 'You'll be the number five this year, mate. If any member of the team can't ride for any reason, you'll take their place. You'll be riding in individual races. And you'll help out in the teams events.'

Flea's cold eyes slid over me like a glacier. He was up to something. I just knew it.

'Now remember,' Gary said, stepping up onto a blue milk crate, 'riding as a team means riding together. Not only is your ability going to be judged, so too is your teamwork, not to mention the presentation of your horses and your tack. But by far the most important criteria for the judges is your TEAMWORK!'

Gary's eyes rested on Carly's for a moment. She wriggled under his gaze.

'So today and every day we train together in our teams as a team. Everybody understand?'

Becky and I nodded. We looked over at Carly, Ryan and Flea. They were huddled together, whispering.

'Check them out,' I whispered to Becky. 'They're like the Three Creepketeers!'

She laughed. 'That's a classic.'

'What do you think they're up to?' I hissed.

Becky shrugged. 'I've got no idea. But if I know them like I think I do, it can't be good.'

'What do you mean?'

Becky leaned forward. 'Carly, Flea, Ryan and me have been in the same team together for years. You show up and Ryan's made number five. That's bad news for us.'

'How come?' I asked, anger growing in my stomach.

'You and my dad are the reasons he's off the team. We'd both better keep an eye on our backs until the gymkhana is over.'

I had another peek at the Creepketeers. They were glaring at us. Flea made a threatening fist and slammed it into his open hand. I shivered. 'Becky?' I said, swallowing. 'Have you got a will?'

'Better than that,' she said, flicking a strand of Charlie's silky black mane over his neck. 'I've got a way.'

'This year we'll be competing in three teams events,' Gary called over the chatter. 'Bending racing, flag racing and barrel racing, which I believe is Ashleigh's speciality.' He winked at me and smiled. 'We'll also have riders competing in individual events.'

I grinned at Becky. She was riding in dressage and

the showjumping event as well as the teams events. Jumping or cross-country, which I really wanted to try, was going to have to wait until next year. Honey and I still needed to really get to know one another. And although Amanda had given us the green light to enter the gymkhana she had made me promise to ride in only one event. So the teams events was it.

'In your teams,' Gary instructed. The riders sorted themselves into groups of four. 'We're going to be training for most of the morning for the teams events, then after lunch we'll have a go at the individual events.'

Gary had set up a bending race on the club's flat, open paddock. There were four long lines of five poles, set up five and a half metres apart. Becky, me, Flea and Carly lined up in front of the Under-12s course. The Under 10s lined up next to us. Julie and Jodie gave me the thumbs up. On the other side, the Under 14s were moving into position. Beside them, the Opens were ready to go.

Gary stepped up on his crate. 'The point of this race is to get through the course without breaking or knocking down any of the poles. The winner is the team with the fastest time that also manages to get through with a clear run. Because this is a team event you'll be passing a baton from one rider to the next.'

Some of the riders groaned.

'You *must* collect the baton from the start line. If you drop the baton, dismount and pick it up. When all four riders are home your time will be recorded.'

We gathered our reins and prepared for the race. Carly was riding first followed by Becky, me and Flea. My heart buzzed with nerves. This was it, our chance to show everyone that we deserved our place on the team, that the try-outs hadn't been a fluke.

Gary stepped down, picked up his crate and jogged out of the way.

'On your marks,' he called.

I tensed up.

'Get set.'

I held my reins high up onto Honey's neck, waiting.

'Go!'

Carly burst out of the starting line on Destiny. She started the course on the left side of the first pole and then bent right and left through the poles until she reached the end pole. She pulled Destiny hard right around it and raced through the course, galloping back to the start line to slap the shiny red baton into Becky's outstretched hand.

Becky and Charlie took the course as neatly and naturally as they did everything else, as though they'd been doing it all their lives.

Carly pulled up on Destiny and sneered. 'Try to beat that ride, Spiller. You don't stand a chance on that nag.'

'Ashleigh!' Becky screamed. She was back already, waving the baton at me. I grabbed it and Honey broke away from the line into a smooth gallop. We bent left around the first pole and Honey galloped away from it. The second appeared and Honey bent right around it. She seemed to know what to do. I gave up on trying to control her and let her make the decisions. We bent around the third and fourth poles then Honey galloped to the fifth and swung tight around it. We made it home in a heartbeat.

I held out the baton to Flea. He made a swipe for it. I let go and it fell to the ground with a horrifying thud.

'Just great!' Flea roared, his face red and shiny. 'You're even more hopeless than I thought.'

I looked around. The other teams were well away. We were the only ones to have dropped the baton.

'Dismount!' Becky screamed. 'Quick. Pick it up!'

'Why don't you be quiet, Rebecca's Garden,' Carly screamed right back. 'If it wasn't for your dumb little friend we would have won!'

'We still can!' I shrieked. 'Flea, pick it up. We can do it!'

He glared at me, then swung his leg over Scud's withers and slid down to the ground. He picked up the baton and shoved it into his back pocket, then mounted again as though he was going out for a nice, relaxing Sunday ride.

'What are you doing?' Becky yelled. 'The Under 14s are already back! The Opens are getting ready for the next event!'

Flea sneered at her and kicked Scud into a gallop and the horse tore through the course like a maniac. The other teams screamed and cheered. Flea crossed the finish line last, but in a record time. The fastest of the day so far. A grin was plastered across his face.

Gary stormed over to us. 'What was that? Fighting during a race! What happened to teamwork?' He turned to Flea, his eyes wild with anger. 'And you? What did you think you were doing?'

Flea shrugged. 'It wasn't my fault. She let go of the baton before I had a good grip on it.'

Flea turned to me, his face twisted into an ugly sneer. 'Call yourself a rider, Spiller?' he spat. 'You couldn't ride your way out of a cardboard box. My dog could take those corners better than you.'

'Enough!' Gary barked.

My face burned with anger and shame. I had never made a mistake in a team race before. I was sure I had put the baton in Flea's hand, but it had all happened so fast.

'Just drop her from the team, Gary,' Carly pleaded. 'We won last year without her. She'll just drag us down.'

'My decision is final. Not negotiable.' Gary slammed his cap over his thick black hair and marched over to the bending course to dump a witch's hat near the last pole with five flags sticking out of it.

'You know how to flag race at least, I hope,' Carly said once Gary was out of earshot.

'Naturally.' I smiled at her, hoping that she couldn't see how scared I was; scared of losing; scared of making an idiot of myself. And right at that moment I was really scared of Carly.

Gary called us to attention. The course was ready. A few minutes later we were lined up again, ready to race.

Carly was away first again on Destiny. Although I hated to admit it, she was a good rider. And Destiny was a great horse. It wasn't fair that she had Carly for an owner. No horse could ever have done anything bad enough to deserve that. Unfortunately Carly wasn't just a good rider, she looked good as well. Her clothes were always perfect. Her boots were always shiny. Her hair was always in that tight cold little bun at the base of her neck. And I hated her. But she made it through the course in good time and dropped her flag into the bucket that was waiting near the start line.

Becky was out next. She galloped straight through the course, turning Charlie neatly around the furthest pole to snatch the flag. The other riders screamed and cheered her on. Gary watched his daughter's every move. Nerves bubbled in my stomach and Honey was tense, like she knew it was almost our turn.

Holding the flag straight up Becky galloped back through the course and dropped it into the bucket.

Honey broke out of the line into a full gallop and went straight down the course. We had to ride the entire course without knocking down any of the poles. My heart thumped. I could hear the shouts of the riders and the thud of Honey's hooves on the earth. She twisted her body left and right, tight around the poles and turned right hard. The flag was there, and Honey slowed for a second as she took the pole. I snatched the flag and flipped my arm backwards, sweeping it up into the air. I gave Honey a free rein and she took us home in a mad rush of speed.

I dropped my flag into the bucket, feeling almost delirious with relief that I'd made it back without a hitch. Flea broke away on Scud. I didn't watch him ride. It didn't matter what happened next. I had done it. Honey had done it. We had proved to everyone there that we were a riding force to be reckoned with. It was one of the best moments of my life. Other than finding out Honey was going to be mine forever.

Flea roared past on Scud, dropping his flag and Carly was out again on Destiny to claim the final flag. I closed my eyes, leaned forward and wrapped my arms around Honey's damp neck, feeling her warmth soak into me.

'You perfect horse,' I murmured to her. 'My perfect Honey horse.'

'Ashleigh!'

My eyes flew open. I sat up and grabbed my reins.

'Ashleigh, we won!' Becky threw her arms around my neck, bouncing in her saddle with excitement. 'And check them out,' she whispered, jerking her head towards the Creepketeers. They had crowded together and were pointing at us, sour looks on their faces. 'You showed them. You showed them good and proper.'

'Thanks.'

'Wait. Isn't that your dad?'

'Where?' I twisted around in my saddle.

'There.' Becky pointed. Sure enough, there he was, leaning against the fence, his arms folded across his chest.

'I don't believe it!' I said, my heart swelling with joy. 'He hardly ever watches me ride.'

The Creepketeers ambled past us. Flea pulled Scud up next to Becky and smirked. 'You may be daddy's girl here, Rebecca's Garden, but just wait till he's not the judge. I'll wipe the ring with you at the gymkhana.'

'I can't wait, Fleabag,' Becky snapped, her anger boiling over.

He laughed and kicked Scud into a canter. Carly and Ryan followed suit. Becky watched them, fuming. Even her long thick plaits looked upset.

'Don't worry, Becky,' I said. 'We'll thrash them. Just wait.'

TWENTY-FIVE

Hacking it Out

'Great idea to go for a ride. I've been so stressed out about the gymkhana, I really needed to get my mind off it.' I patted Honey's firm golden neck.

'She's looking good,' Becky said. 'Must be all the extra training sessions.' She drummed her heels on Charlie's middle and he broke into a neat trot. Even when he was relaxing, Charlie was perfect.

We rode for a while, side by side along the soft grassy roadside, not speaking. The horses' hooves padded on the path. Magpies yodelled in the treetops. An occasional car chugged past. But otherwise it was still, and quiet.

The gymkhana was only a week away and both

of us were feeling the pressure. We'd built an arena to practise in on the flat, open paddock at my place and trained every day after school. Flea hadn't trained at all. He was too busy sitting on his fence watching us ride and laughing his guts up. He'd actually fallen off it a few times.

'How's Horse Cents going?'

I moaned. 'I'm nearly out of ideas. There are only so many times you can wash your mum's car. She reckons I'll wash the paint off eventually. I've actually started collecting cans.'

'Did you manage to pay Amanda?'

'Finally, yes,' I sighed. 'I got a job grooming some of the horses from Riding Club. Twenty bucks for a full groom, thirty to shampoo, dry and groom. Most of them went for the thirty-dollar package. I was wrecked after that, but some of them told me it would be a regular gig.'

Becky frowned. 'Why can't they just groom their own horses? I would never let anyone else groom Charlie.' She smiled sheepishly. 'Except you, of course.'

I shrugged and pulled Honey clear of a bundle of dry fallen branches that could get caught around her leg. 'Heaps of reasons. Homework, dancing lessons, and Sandra from the Under 10s is actually allergic to Chocolate.'

'I've got it!' Becky shrieked suddenly. Charlie's ears flicked.

'You've got what?'

'The perfect plan. The best idea. It's amazing. I'm a genius!' Her eyes sparkled.

'What? What?'

'Have you ever made a ribbon browband?'

'For a bridle? Yeah. So?'

'Make some. SELL them. Start a business! My aunty owns a fabric shop. She's always sending us off-cuts. You'll make enough money to keep Honey in golden horseshoes for the rest of her life!'

'Do you reckon?'

'Yeah, of course. Sell them at Riding Club. Set up a stall at the gymkhana!'

I grinned.

This was possibly the best moneymaking idea so far. 'Becky, you are brilliant.'

'I know,' she gushed. 'And you can call your business "Ashleigh's Browbands".'

I let the name bounce around inside my head. It

sounded funny. 'That's a bit of a mouthful. How about "Bandies"?'

She laughed. 'Cool as.'

We slapped our hands together. Just then, I noticed something.

'Becky, pull up.'

Becky reined Charlie in. I dismounted and handed her Honey's reins.

'What's going on?'

'I never thought I'd end up doing this, but until Bandies takes off, I need all the money I can get. Honey eats like a horse.' I pointed to a pile of squashed, multicoloured soft drink cans.

Some were brand new. Some were half-buried in the mud. Some were playing host to trails of ants. Reefing them out of the sludge with my bare hands was disgusting, but love for a horse does strange things to you.

'Great idea!' Becky said, nodding her approval. 'We should collect everything we see. You'll make money and we'll clean up Shady Creek at the same time.'

I tiptoed around the pile of cans and checked under bushes and over the fence. There was at least five bucks' worth right here in this one spot. 'I just need something to carry them in.'

I found a plastic shopping bag tangled around a shrub and grabbed it. Within minutes it was full and I was counting dollars in my head.

'That should do for now,' I said, wiping my hands down the front of my old jodhpurs. I tied the bag in a knot and looped it around my wrist, taking the reins from Becky at the same time. Honey stepped backwards. She'd never done that before.

'Stand!' I said to her. I gripped the pommel and the bag and prepared myself to spring into the saddle. As I bounced I noticed Honey's eyes rolling back.

'She seems nervous about something,' Becky said.

I landed in the saddle and pushed my right foot into the stirrup while I shook my reins down Honey's neck.

The plastic bag full of soft drink cans clanked against Honey's shoulder. I felt her body tense underneath me. It felt like she was curling up into a ball, a huge tight ball of horse.

'What's going on?' Becky said.

'I'm getting off.'

I slid my feet out of the stirrups as a gust of wind swirled leaves up around us. I could feel Honey's mouth through the reins, hard and tense. She danced on her forelegs, tossed her head and laid her ears back, flat.

'Ashleigh, dismount!' Becky watched in horror as my horse transformed from her usual calm self into a terror-struck maniac.

The bag jostled against Honey's shoulder with a scrunch, and she burst into a bolt, galloping down the road with me still on her back, without my stirrups, the cans thumping against her side. I let go of the bag and it and its contents were mangled by her churning legs. At the touch of the bag, Honey bucked in fear. It was the bag, the plastic bag! That was what had spooked her. You idiot, I thought as I fought for control. You were so caught up with money you couldn't see what the bag was doing to your horse!

I gripped with my knees and held on tight to the pommel with one hand, reining her in with the other. It wasn't working. She wasn't slowing down. I tried again. Honey exploded into a mad series of pig-roots, thrashing her head and legs. The reins were jerked out of my hands and they flipped over Honey's head.

I opened my mouth and screamed, wrapping my arms around Honey's neck. There was so much that could go wrong. I could slip underneath Honey and be mashed like a boiled potato by those hooves. All I could do was wait for it to finish.

'Ashleigh!'

I peered out to the side and noticed a flash of brown. It was Charlie, with Becky on board, one hand reaching out towards me.

'Hold on!' Becky screamed. 'I'll try and pull her up.'

Becky reined Charlie over so that he was head to head with Honey. She leaned across and made a swipe for my reins.

'Help me, Becky!'

The reins spun like a propeller, around and around under Honey's neck. Becky reached over, out of her saddle, but she missed the reins again.

'Hang on!' Becky called to me. 'She'll tire herself out.'

Charlie pulled up level with Honey again. Becky reached across, holding tight to her pommel and made another grab for the reins. But it was hopeless. Honey had no intention of doing anything but bolting, even if it meant killing the pair of us in the process.

'Ashleigh, look out!' Becky screamed as she dropped back, out of Honey's way. I peeked over Honey's shoulder. A ditch was looming ahead of us and I prepared for a fall. The ditch rushed forward. Honey hesitated, then sprang from her hind legs and soared over it. I felt myself falling, and I tried to relax, which was pretty difficult seeing that certain death was imminent. But after my experience with Scud I knew that my chances of breaking every bone in my body were less if I curled up and rolled when I hit the ground. There was a terrible moment of being in mid-air, then I crashed to the ground.

'Ashleigh, are you okay?' Becky pulled up on Charlie and scrambled off.

I lay still with my eyes closed, sharp pain thudding through me. 'Where's Honey?' I gasped.

I felt something soft and wet nuzzle my cheek. 'Becky, cut it out, can't you see I'm in pain?' I groaned.

Becky laughed with relief. 'It's not me. No way I'd be kissing you, the state you're in. With all the mud and leaves you look like a giant lamington!'

My eyes flew open. I looked up into Honey's face. She nuzzled me again.

I managed to reach up to rub her nose.

'The next time you decide to freak out, could you at least give me time to find my stirrups?'

'Nice one, Spiller! That was the funniest thing I've ever seen!'

I gawked in disbelief. Flea and Scud were watching from the other side of the road. I wished I had been knocked unconscious. At least I wouldn't have known he was there.

'Y'really are a loser,' he roared.

'We'll see who the loser is next week, Fleabag!' Becky shrieked.

He cantered away, laughing his head off.

I was furious. He'd managed to make me look like an idiot for the last time. I wasn't going to let him win ever again. I knew that I had to smash him. And the gymkhana was the place to do it.

TWENTY-SIX

Horse Proud

'I'm proud of all of you. No matter how we do tomorrow, just remember that Shady Creek Riding Club is the best in this district, if not the whole country!' Gary shielded his eyes with his hand and smiled.

Becky and I grinned at each other and clasped hands. Some of the riders cheered.

'So, with that in mind you'd better bring home truckloads of ribbons or I'll hunt you down and tie you to the flagpole at the showground.'

I laughed aloud. Becky flushed with humiliation. She was in agony whenever Gary cracked dumb jokes.

Our last training session at Riding Club before the gymkhana was over. Gary dismissed us early. Becky and I rode out of the gate together.

'Been a great morning, huh?' I said.

She nodded. 'Especially for you. How many browbands did you sell?'

'One to everyone except the Creepketeers and three to your dad. At five bucks apiece that comes to ...' I paused and did a quick calculation in my head. 'A hundred dollars!'

'That'll keep Honey in feed for a while.'

I smiled and relaxed. I felt like I didn't have to worry about the problem of paying for Honey's upkeep for a few weeks at least. And more money would come my way at the gymkhana. Hundreds of people would want browbands there.

We stopped outside my place.

'I'll see you first thing,' Becky said. 'We'll be here at six sharp with the horse float, so be ready!'

I grinned at her. 'See ya!'

She cantered down the road and disappeared around the corner. Honey trotted down the driveway and into the corral, where she knew a drink and a feed were waiting for her. I untacked her and dried her off, then turned her out into the back paddock for a roll and a graze. I would have to set up the horse beauty parlour later to get her looking spectacular for the gymkhana, but for now, she deserved a rest.

I watched her for a while then jogged up to the house and let myself in the back door. Mum was in the kitchen making herself a cup of tea.

'Want one?' she said, holding up a dry teabag. It spun around in mid-air like a music box ballerina.

I shook my head and flopped into a chair. She sat opposite me and grinned. She was glimmering. Her eyes were sparkly. There was colour in her cheeks. She looked like her old self for the first time in months.

'What's going on?'

Mum took a sip of tea. 'I have some news.'

'Not again!' I buried my face in my hands. We were definitely moving back to the city this time. Dad would have to find another job. I would have to leave Becky behind. And as for Honey? I couldn't bear to think about it. They'd done it to me once and I wasn't going to let it happen again. I stood up, bristling.

'I just want you to know that I'm staying here.'

Mum spluttered into her cup. 'What?'

I folded my arms. 'I said I'm staying here. I'm not moving again. I'll live with Becky. I can sleep in her room.'

Mum smiled. 'What are you talking about?'

I sat down again, confused. 'We're not moving?'

'No.'

'So what's your news?'

Mum's face lit up. She grabbed my hands and squeezed them. 'I got a job, possum. You don't have to worry any more.'

'Worry?'

'About money! About fundraising. We can take care of Honey's expenses now.'

Shock seeped into my stomach. My head spun. 'Where? When?'

'At a small company in Pinebark Ridge. It's about a fifteen-minute drive from here.'

I looked into her eyes, hoping she was telling me the truth. Especially about the money part. 'When do you start?'

'Tomorrow!' She laughed aloud with pleasure and

rubbed her hands together. 'I can't wait to tell your father.'

'Gymkhana day.'

'I'm so sorry, Ashleigh. I know what it means to you, but I have to take this job. Be happy for me!'

'I am.'

I was happy for her, but unhappy for me. Nobody would be there to see me ride. And in my very first gymkhana with Honey. I could feel the tears welling up behind my eyes, but I didn't want to cry in front of her.

I stood up and walked out of the kitchen.

'You know, I saw a bit of your ride today.'

I stopped at the doorway. 'How?'

'I was watching.' Mum took a sip of tea and smiled over her cup.

I frowned. 'I saw Dad at the end, but I didn't see you.'

'You never do.'

'What do you mean, I never do?'

Mum laughed and set her cup down carefully in its saucer. 'I always watch you. You're just so caught up in your riding you've never noticed.' She picked up a sweet biscuit and took a bite.

'Are you sure?' I felt horrible. I'd always thought she didn't care about the one thing that meant everything to me.

'Don't worry,' Mum said. 'That's what makes you a good rider. It's like it's just you and the horse.' She smiled and traced her finger around the mouth of the teacup. 'It's really something.'

I slipped onto her lap and wrapped my arms tight around her neck. It had been ages since we'd shared a hug. It felt great.

'By the way, there's a letter for you.' She took a small white envelope out of her pocket and handed it to me. I turned it over and read the return address on the back. It was from Jenna. I ran upstairs to my room and closed the door. I sat on my bed, holding the envelope. My hands were shaking. We were supposed to be best friends forever, but it seemed like years since I'd seen her. Did she have a new best friend? Was it possible to have two best friends at once?

I tore open the envelope, wondering why Jenna had sent me a letter by snail mail and not email. It had to mean something, but what?

I unfolded the neat white square of paper inside and read.

Dear Ash,

I know you must be wondering why I've written you a letter. Well I know that you and computers aren't the best mix and from what I've heard, if you get anywhere near the Net, you might buy another horse!

Besides, you're probably heaps too busy practising for the contest and looking after your horse to even think about emails.

I just wanted to wish you good luck for your big day. I hope we can see each other again soon.

By the way, thanks for that email you sent.

Love, Jenna.
PS. I miss you too, heaps.

I read the letter again and again. I had so many questions. How did Jenna find out about Jester? How did she know about the gymkhana?

I folded it up again and pushed it back into the envelope, determined to focus on the gymkhana, which was less than twenty-four hours away. I jogged down the stairs and outside to groom Honey.

TWENTY-SEVEN

Horse Beautiful

'Horses?'

I twisted around in the back seat of the Chos' car and peered through the rear window at the horse float. Honey and Charlie were still on board. 'Check.'

'Tack?' Becky had her eyes closed, trying to remember everything we needed for the gymkhana.

I felt for the saddles and bridles in the back compartment. 'Check.'

'Video camera?'

'It's on the seat. Next to you.'

'Riders?'

'Duh.'

Becky laughed. 'Okay, um, Bandies?'

I nodded and patted a bag at my feet. 'A wide assortment of Bandies to suit the needs and tastes of every rider.'

Becky's eyes widened. 'You must have been awake all night thinking up that one!'

'Tell me about it,' I groaned. 'I could hardly sleep.'

'Me too.' Becky stared out of the window at the shadows. It was early. The sun was only just poking up over the horizon.

'I was never this worried at home. It's all this business with the Creepketeers.' It was true. Despite the performances that Honey and I had been turning in at Riding Club I was packing death. I had to prove to them that we had what it took. Mostly, though, I had to prove it to myself.

We pulled into the car park at the Shady Creek and Districts Showground. Although it was early, there were horses, cars, trucks and different coloured horse floats everywhere. A frowning attendant, who looked like she'd rather still be in bed, waved us towards a space under a big oak tree. Gary parked the car and we tumbled out into the crisp morning air to unload and tether the horses.

Honey was gleaming from the hours I had spent the day before shampooing and grooming her. She had spent the night in a New Zealand rug although the weather was mild. It had kept her clean and free of her usual morning mane and tail full of leaves and twigs from rolling and rubbing against the trees. I had painted her hooves, trimmed the long hairs at the back of her legs and plaited her tail all the way to the bottom.

'I guess we should get started on their hair.' Becky smiled at me and dumped a crate full of brushes and horse beauty products between us.

I snipped off the elastic band holding the plait in place and shook out Honey's tail.

'What did you plait her tail for?' Becky asked.

'Makes it look fuller.'

'Oh.' Becky turned back to Charlie's rump. We didn't have a lot to say. We were too nervous. The best thing to do was concentrate on getting our horses looking their absolute best.

I braided Honey's golden tail to the bottom of her dock, the tailbone, and wove the hair into a long plait, looping it underneath the braid and securing it with a thread. I sprayed the finished job with hair spray and stepped back to admire my handiwork.

'Looks great!' Becky enthused. 'I had no idea you could do that.'

'There's a lot you don't know about me.' I grabbed a water spray bottle out of the crate.

I divided Honey's mane into nine equal bunches, winding elastic bands around each to hold them in place. I plaited each bunch and sewed them into neat balls. Her mane looked fantastic. I felt more excited and nervous when I saw her all done up. It was really happening. The gymkhana was only a few hours away.

'I don't believe it. Ashleigh Miller,' said a voice.

I spun around. I couldn't believe it either. 'What are you doing here?' I gasped.

Nicki King scowled at me from underneath an expensive-looking black riding helmet and folded her arms. Her cool eyes slid over Honey. 'So this is your horse?'

I nodded tightly and placed a protective hand on Honey's rump, glancing at Becky who had a look of utter confusion on her face.

'I guess we'll be competing,' Nicki said, taking in Becky, Charlie and the float in one distasteful stare.

'Guess so. How's Sonny?' I asked, remembering the gorgeous Thoroughbred gelding Nicki's parents had bought her just before I moved to Shady Creek.

'Sold him. He was useless,' Nicki sniped.

Becky's mouth dropped open into a big O.

'So what are you riding?' I said.

'New horse. She's an Arab. This is our first gymkhana together.'

'Good luck, Nicki.' I hoped she would get the hint and go in search of someone else to torture.

'I won't need it. I'm riding an Arab.' Nicki lifted her chin and gave Honey a look so snooty that my fists curled into angry bunches. 'And the instruction I'm getting at City Stables makes South Beach look like a joke. So if anyone needs luck, it's you.'

Nicki turned and walked towards a man who was grooming a silver-coloured mare with a perfect, dished Arab face.

'Don't tell me you're friends with her!' Becky spluttered.

'Get serious. Nicki and I were never friends. She's a total snob.' I rummaged in the crate for a cloth and some hoof oil. 'Sounds like she left South Beach Stables. Holly must have chucked a party.'

'Who knows,' Becky mused. 'If the Creeps ever leave Shady Creek we'll be chucking one of our own.' Becky put the finishing touches on Charlie's thick black mane. Making sure Honey's hooves were clean, I painted them again with black hoof oil and the job was complete. Honey looked like a champion. All we needed now was the ribbon.

'Today's the day, everyone,' Gary said. The riders competing for Shady Creek Riding Club gathered around him for what Becky called 'the pep talk'.

'He says the same thing every year,' she had whispered earlier. It was the first time I'd heard it, so I was all ears.

'This is what we've been preparing for. All our training comes down to how we do today, so I'd like you to all put in a top effort. As we're here representing Shady Creek Riding Club we'll all be on our very best behaviour.'

Was it my imagination, or was Gary looking right at the Creepketeers?

'So,' he continued, 'let me remind you of gymkhana etiquette. That's manners,' he added, noticing the blank looks on some of the riders' faces.

'Here we go again,' Flea mumbled.

'Firstly, be at your event on time. Be polite to the judges and other competitors. Pay attention to and carry out the instructions that are given to you.'

Carly rolled her eyes. 'Will there be a test on this?'

Gary smiled. 'Not a test. But there will be an essay. Now, if you don't mind, I'd like to continue.'

Carly glowered and exhaled sharply.

'Look after your horses. Don't ride in the crowd. Congratulate the winners of your events. Don't leave the ring until you're told to do so.' Gary crammed his hands into his pockets and frowned. 'Have I forgotten anything?'

'The judging isn't finished until all the ribbons are given out,' Julie and Jodie said in unison. Laughter rippled through the riders.

'Have I said this before?'

'Only every year!' Becky moaned.

'Okay, well don't forget that Ring One is Western, Ring Two is English, Ring Three is Junior Riders and Novelty, and Ring Four is Beginners.

Most of you will be riding in Rings Two, Three and Four. Flea is the only rider to be competing in any Western riding events.'

I turned around, surprised, and stared at Flea. I had no idea before that he was a Western rider, but it did explain his riding style.

'Make sure you know which ring you're in,' Gary chattered. He seemed more nervous than we were. 'Just a few more words and I'll leave you to it.'

'No, please, I can't take any more!' Flea cried, falling to his knees.

'At the end of the day being a good sport and doing your very best is the most important thing. So go out there, do your best and win.' Gary grinned. 'And, good luck!'

It was almost time for the first events to begin. Becky and I made a beeline for our horses. I heard the scream before I saw anything.

'I don't believe it!' Becky wailed.

People gathered around, curious to see what the fuss was about.

'My horse! Who did this to my horse?' Becky sat in a pile of leaves, buried her face in her hands and sobbed.

Charlie was a mess. His tail had been unbraided and was a tangled black clump of sticks and leaves. Mud was smeared down his legs like a thick layer of peanut butter. The quarter markings that Becky had combed into his coat had been rubbed out.

Honey looked just as bad. I stood dead still on the spot as though I was glued to it. My beautiful champion horse looked like a wild brumby. The rosettes I had so carefully braided into her mane had been pulled out and she looked as though someone had emptied a bucket of dirt over her. I wanted to cry.

Becky *was* crying. 'What am I going to do, Ashleigh?' she said. 'My first event starts in twenty minutes, and it's *dressage!*'

'Who could do such a thing?' I groaned.

'Who do you reckon?' Becky said. 'The Creepketeers!'

'Don't worry, we can fix it if we work together.'

'Do you think so?'

I grabbed our crate and rummaged for some sponges, brushes and a currycomb. 'I'll do the mud, you do his mane.'

★ ★ ★

Somehow we managed to do it. Fifteen minutes after we'd started, Becky emerged from the horse float where she had changed into a pair of new white jodhpurs, a black jacket, a white shirt, tie and gloves and long black riding boots. With her hair wound into a neat bun, and her spotless silk-covered black helmet, she looked stunning.

'Wow,' I said, staring at her.

'Wow,' she said, staring at Charlie.

'I'll walk you to the ring.'

Becky nodded, breathless with nerves. I stroked Honey's muzzle. She still looked terrible, but I had heaps of time before my first event to come back and fix up the damage.

Becky lined up with four other riders, including Carly, at the dressage arena for her test. Carly's face turned the colour of cottage cheese when she saw Becky. She obviously hadn't counted on seeing her at all, much less looking as hot as she did.

I sat down and watched Becky and Charlie perform their test. It was only about five minutes long, but I could tell that it was hard work and that they were under pressure. Dressage had never been my thing for precisely that reason. I was in it for fun, not for stress! But their performance was so amazing that even I was spellbound. It was no surprise to me at all when Becky won the blue ribbon. I cheered louder than anyone else in the stands, especially at the look on Carly's face when a green third-place ribbon was fixed to Destiny's bridle by one of the judges. That look was nearly worth the mess we'd cleaned up.

I scrambled down the stand to meet Becky as she came out of the ring. She saw me and dismounted, her face flushed with excitement and relief. I hugged her hard.

'Congratulations!' I said. 'You deserve it.'

'If the Pathetic Loser Club has finished its meeting, could you get out of my way?'

Becky and I stared up at Carly.

'Well done,' I said. 'Third place is pretty good. Considering how distracted you must have been by messing up our horses.'

'Just try and prove it.'

'I intend to.' I smiled.

Carly ignored me and glared at Becky. 'I'll smash you in the jumping, Rebecca's Garden,' she muttered, and kicked Destiny into a trot through the crowd.

'She's not supposed to do that, is she?'

Becky sighed. 'Carly does a lot of things she's not supposed to do. Let's get back to Honey and see how she's going.'

We walked Charlie back through the showground towards the float where Honey was still tethered. I could hear a horse whinnying. There were shouts and suddenly, the sickening thud of horseshoes on metal.

'Something's wrong,' I said, a terrible feeling swelling in my stomach.

'You run ahead. I have to walk Charlie. It's the rules,' Becky said. 'I'll be there as soon as I can.'

I broke into a sprint and ran through the crowds of people; couples strolling hand in hand, toddlers in strollers, riders dressed up for their events. I ran past the Western Ring, past the cafeteria, past the home-made jam stall and towards the float. The whinnying grew shrill and more panicked. I pushed my way through the adults crowding around the Chos' float, wishing I could see over their heads.

Honey was shrieking in panic, thrashing her head and rearing, her forelegs flailing dangerously close to the float. There was a huge ugly dent in the side of Gary's car.

What could have spooked her?

Plastic bags.

Someone had tied at least a dozen plastic bags to the float. I ripped them down and threw them inside the float. There were only three people in the world who knew that plastic bags spooked Honey, and I could cross two off the list immediately!

I took a step towards Honey and reached out my hand. Someone grabbed my shoulder.

'Get back from there!' yelled a man in an official-looking jacket. 'That horse is crazy. I've got a good mind to eliminate her from today's gymkhana.'

I shook my shoulder free. 'She's not crazy. She's terrified!'

He backed off, holding his hands up in surrender. I turned back to Honey. Her nostrils were flaring and she was breathing hard, yanking on the lead rope and trying to break free.

'Easy!' I said. 'Honey, it's me, Ashleigh.'

Honey reared and struck out with her forelegs. Her hoof clipped the window of the horse float.

I took another step. 'Honey, go easy. It's okay.' I touched her shoulder. She calmed a little.

'Typical,' sneered a familiar voice. Nicki King sauntered over; holding her nose up so high I was surprised she could see what was going on at all. 'Typical bitzer horse. A purebred would never carry on like that!'

'Get lost, Nicki!' I snapped, backing away a little from Honey's thrashing forelegs.

'It's a good thing you moved away from the city. You could never become a member of a decent stable with–'

'Ashleigh, be careful!' Becky cried, pushing Nicki out of the way.

'How *dare* you!' Nicki sucked in her breath and brushed at her sleeves with a gloved hand.

The man I'd seen grooming her silver Arab tapped her gingerly on the shoulder. 'Jewel is ready for you, Miss King.'

'Lucky for you,' Nicki spat. She glared at Becky then disappeared into the crowd.

'Everything's all right, Becky. Isn't it, Honey?' I took another step and ran my hand down Honey's face. She settled. I pulled the rope free and rubbed under her forelock. She relaxed enough for me to lead her to the other side of the float. I wrapped my arms around her neck.

'I'm so sorry, Honey!' I whispered. 'I should never have left you alone!' I tethered her again, using a slipknot, and checked her for injuries. Apart from being sweaty and distressed, she was okay. But I was furious! Flea was the only one apart from Becky who knew about Honey's fear of plastic bags. I was going to get the Creepketeers if it was the last thing I did.

TWENTY-EIGHT

Flea, Spies and Videotape

'Julie, Jodie,' I hissed. 'Now!'

The twins peered out of the door of Becky's father's float where I was hiding and stepped outside. I poked Becky's video camera through the window and pressed the red record button. The tape whirred as it began to roll. I squinted through the lens, wishing I were invisible.

They had been briefed. They knew what their mission was. This was between good and evil. Right and wrong. Us and them — the Creepketeers.

My pulse throbbed in my head. My stomach squeezed with nerves. My mouth was as dry as the Simpson Desert.

Julie looked over her shoulder at me and winked, then spoke loudly to her sister.

'So, Jodie, that Ashleigh Miller. I would do anything to see her lose today.'

Jodie nodded. 'Yeah, um, I reckon she should never have been allowed on the team. She'll bring them down for sure.'

If I hadn't told them exactly what to say I would have been hurt. But their talk achieved the desired effect. Flea sidled over in no time.

'So,' he said, chewing on a piece of grass. 'Don't youse like her either?'

The twins shook their heads.

'Nah,' Jodie boomed. 'She's really annoying.'

Flea looked at her closely, his eyebrows knotted together. 'Wotcha yelling for? I'm not deaf.'

Jodie turned to her twin, panic etched on her face. If she blew it, they would be on Flea's hit list as well. This had to work. It was my only chance to prove he had set Honey up.

'Sorry,' she stammered. 'I was listening to this really loud music last night. I didn't realise I was talking so loud.'

'S'okay.' Flea smirked. 'How would you like to help me fix her once and for all?'

'Who?'

'Jodie, what's wrong with ya?' Flea snapped. 'Ashleigh Miller, that's who!'

'Oh,' she said. 'Yeah. I'd love to get her.' She tucked a wisp of loose hair behind her ear and shifted from one foot to another, looking over her shoulder.

'Here's the plan,' he said, his eyes bright. 'Before the teams events we loosen her girth. She'll wind up under that nag's belly before she makes it around the first barrel!'

I shuddered. I had no idea he hated me that much.

'How do we know you can pull it off?' Jodie said. 'I mean, we don't want to get caught.'

Flea laughed. 'Are you kiddin'? Didn't yer see her horse before the dressage test? Or Becky's? We totally wrecked 'em.'

Julie looked over her shoulder at the float. Jodie poked her and smiled at Flea.

'So, you don't happen to know who did that plastic bag thing, do you?' she said. I wanted to puke. 'I mean, that was so clever. We were really impressed.'

Flea beamed. My guts writhed like a bag full of snakes. 'That was me! Smart, huh!'

Jodie's eyes were full of admiration. She was really getting into it. 'Wow! You did that all by yourself?'

'Ryan helped a bit,' he boasted. 'But it was my idea.'

I switched off the video camera and slumped on the floor of the float. I didn't want to hear any more.

But I had what I needed.

'You look cheerful,' Becky said. She had changed into her Shady Creek Riding Club uniform.

'What are you doing now?'

'Jumping.' She shortened her stirrups and checked her tack. 'What about you?'

'The teams events aren't until after lunch, so I've got some serious business to do.'

Becky smiled at me over her saddle. 'Bandies?'

'You betcha.' I held up my bag.

Becky's face darkened. 'What about Honey?'

'She's being horse-sat by Julie and Jodie.'

We walked towards Ring Two where the jumping events were about to start.

'So, why are you so happy? You were miserable an hour ago.'

I pulled the miniature videotape out of my pocket. 'Let's just say the Creepketeers are in trouble.'

'Intriguing,' she said, smiling. 'You have to tell me everything.'

We stopped at the marshalling area. Becky sprang into the saddle. Carly was already mounted on Destiny and warming up over a course of trotting poles.

'Good luck!' I said.

Becky nodded and pulled Charlie towards the trotting poles. I opened my bag of Bandies and pulled a dozen out. There were browbands in red and gold, green and yellow, blue and silver and purple and pink, in fact, just about every colour combination I could come up with. All made from Becky's aunty's off-cuts.

'How much?'

I looked up. A girl who looked a few years older than me was standing close by, admiring the collection of Bandies.

'Five dollars each. Or three for ten dollars.'

She dug around the pocket of her jacket and pulled out a ten-dollar note. 'Three, please.'

I pushed the money into my pocket while she chose a few.

It wasn't long before I had another customer, then another and another. Bandies were hot property. I had money in my pocket and a videotape that would expose the biggest scandal in the history of Shady Creek Riding Club. There was only one more thing I wanted. A blue ribbon. Or three!

TWENTY-NINE

Every Horse has Her Day

'Becky, that's unreal!' I held the smooth blue satin ribbon between my fingers.

She shrugged. 'It's okay.'

'Okay?' I was exasperated. 'It's brilliant. You're brilliant. First place in dressage and jumping! You'll be age champion for sure.'

Becky's face turned crimson. 'You ready?'

'Yep.'

Honey was looking as good as she had in the morning. She was calm and seemed to have forgotten all about the plastic bag incident. I held her reins under her chin and led her towards Ring Three. I was a mess this time. My stomach bubbled with nerves. Cold sweat ran in thin streams down my sides.

'You'll be okay,' Becky said.

I nodded, wishing more than ever that Mum and Dad were here to see me ride, that the Creepketeers would develop permanent amnesia and forget to be creeps and that Nicki King was back in the city where she belonged.

We gathered with the other teams in the marshalling area of Ring Three. Flea and Carly were there. They spoke urgently to each other. Ryan was on standby, watching Becky and me with a stony face like one of those guards at Buckingham Palace.

'Whatever you do, don't take your eyes off your tack,' I whispered. Becky gave me the thumbs up. I had filled her in on all the details of the videotape over lunch.

I checked and re-checked my girth. I didn't want to wind up staring up at Honey's belly before I'd even made it to the first barrel.

A man stood up to speak to the Under 12s Teams Events riders. I recognised him as the official who'd wanted to disqualify Honey. My heart thumped. He shot me a disapproving look.

'We'll begin today with the bending race, followed by the flag, and finish up with the barrel. I trust that you know which team you're riding for and the order you're riding in. The first race will begin in two minutes.'

There were six teams competing. They huddled together in their groups of four, whispering to each other, and finishing with a huge high-five. I strained for a glimpse of Nicki and her Arab, but they were nowhere to be seen. The Shady Creek Riding Club Under 12s team sat mounted on their horses in absolute silence. I sat in the saddle, worrying. Had they done anything to set me up? Had they done anything to Honey? I checked her from the top of her head to the tip of her tail, but as I had learned, with the Creepketeers anything was possible. Did they have anything planned? Would I still be alive to tell the tale?

The race began. Carly was out first. The crowd began to cheer. Destiny sprang into a full gallop and tore down the field towards the first pole. I looked over at the other teams. One girl in a red jumper was trying desperately to stop her horse from spinning in circles while the other team members shouted and wailed. Another rider had hit a pole on the first turn.

Carly galloped across the start line, slamming the baton into Becky's hand. Charlie burst into a gallop. I rocked back and forth in the saddle, squelching with nerves. I licked my lips and gripped my reins so hard I could feel my fingernails digging into the palms of my hands.

Becky made a clear run. She galloped towards me, her face flushed with the exhilaration of speed and of coming first. She stretched out her hand, offering me the baton. I snatched it as though it was a bar of solid gold. Honey leapt out over the start line. We galloped towards the first pole. Honey bent slightly left around it, then right around the second, left around the third and right around the fourth. The fifth loomed ahead, only a second or two away. Honey had to make a complete turn around it, keeping her body close, but not knocking down the pole. She slowed a little, twisted her body and rounded it perfectly. We galloped back through the poles and over the line. I held out the baton.

Flea was ready. He wrenched it from my hand and kicked Scud hard. Although the horse was tired from the morning's Western riding events he made off like his name down the course, bending neatly left and right until finally he crossed the finish line a nose in front of the team from Pinebark Ridge. We waited for the announcement.

'First place winner — Shady Creek Riding Club.'

Becky screamed. 'Yes! We did it.'

We hugged each other, laughing. I felt unreal, like my old self. The way I had felt at South Beach Stables on Princess. It was good to be back.

'If you two are over it, we'd better get ready for the flag race,' Carly said.

'Same order as before,' Flea said. 'And ya'd better deliver, Spiller.'

'You can count on it!' I said through clenched teeth, desperately fighting off the desire to wring his ugly neck.

An orange witch's hat with five flags in it had been placed behind the last pole. An empty upturned barrel sat in front of the first. As rider one, Carly would be out twice.

'Hey,' she said suddenly. There was less than a minute to go. 'I don't want to go out first.'

'What are you talking about?' I said.

Carly turned Destiny around. There was thirty seconds to go.

'What do you think you're doing?' Becky yelled.

'It's okay,' I said. 'I'll go out first.'

Becky tugged at my sleeve. 'Are you sure?'

'Yes.' Twenty seconds to go.

'But you'll have to go out . . .' she began.

'Yeah, twice. I know. Don't worry, we'll kick it!'

Honey moved into the first position. Carly took my spot as third rider. Ten seconds to go.

I watched the flags. Five flags. I had to bring home two of them. If I dropped one, we'd be eliminated and I'd be dead meat. If I brought them both home and we won, my future in Shady Creek looked great.

The buzzer rang out and Honey stormed out over the line, springing from her hindquarters into a full gallop. She raced down the course, turning tight around the last pole. I snatched a flag and swung it backwards the way that Holly had taught me at South Beach. One hand was out of action. I had to get Honey back through the course and close enough to the empty barrel to drop the flag in with the other. She galloped back through the course. The crowd cheered me on. I could see Becky at the starting line, ready to go. The wind rushed past my ears and my heart sang. We zoomed past the barrel. I dropped the flag in with a clang and Charlie broke off the mark into a gallop.

I lined up behind Flea and Scud and patted Honey's neck. She had done so well. No matter what the end result was, I was proud of her. We'd proved to everyone that we were champions.

Becky dropped her flag into the barrel and crossed the line. Carly completed the course to claim her flag. It was Flea's turn. I watched the other teams. Only Pinebark Ridge was even close to Flea. If I could keep up the momentum we would win the race hands down.

I held my reins tight, high up on Honey's neck, and prepared to burst out over the line. Honey pawed the ground impatiently. Flea dropped his flag into the barrel. As soon as Scud's sleek black body crossed the line I let my reins loose, giving Honey her head. I trusted her. She knew what to do.

The last rider for Pinebark Ridge was out as well. We were neck and neck from the first pole, down the course to the second and the third. I kept my eyes on that flag, the last one. I just had to get it in the barrel before them and we'd win it. I could hear Becky screaming from the line. Honey's hooves pelted against the earth in time with my heartbeat. The last flag was just within reach. I snatched at it. The rider from Pinebark Ridge was also reaching out. Keep your eyes on the flag, I thought. Keep your eyes on the hand taking the flag. Forget about the other teams. I felt the flag, cool and smooth in my fingertips. Honey surged forward beneath me.

Too fast! I thought.

Too fast! I'm going to lose it.

Honey turned tight around the pole. I wrenched at the flag but, as she galloped back towards the finishing line, I felt it slip from my fingers. I grabbed at it desperately, but it fell. We were eliminated. Pinebark Ridge crossed the line first.

I pulled Honey up, dismounted and grabbed the flag, scrambled back into the saddle and galloped over the finish line.

I felt sick. All our training had been wasted. We'd lost the blue ribbon, thanks to me.

'That was a great ride, Ashleigh,' Becky said as we waited for the barrel race. We had dismounted to give the horses a rest.

'It sucked,' I groaned. 'I'm really sorry, Becky.'

Becky put her arm around my shoulders. 'It was just bad luck.'

'What is it with you and falls, Spiller?' I turned around.

Flea and Carly were standing there, arms folded.

'Yeah.' Carly was red-faced and breathing heavily. 'We lost all because of you!'

'Just wait, Spiller,' Flea hissed. I looked into his eyes and I didn't like what I saw. 'You are so dead.'

I sprang into the saddle. 'I don't think so.'

'You reckon?' Carly snapped.

I nodded. 'Yeah. I do.' I gathered my reins. 'Once Gary sees the little home movie I made earlier you'll be out of Shady Creek Riding Club before you can say sabotage.'

Becky laughed. 'They'd have to be able to spell it first!'

Flea and Carly looked at each other.

'What are you going on about now?' he said.

'I'd really love to tell you, but the barrel race is starting in under a minute, so you might just have to wait until the trial.'

Flea swallowed and made a grab for Scud's reins. Carly scrambled onto Destiny's back.

The barrel race was my favourite. Three barrels set up in a triangle shape, nine metres apart. It was the best fun. As Holly had always said, barrel racing is life. The rest is just details.

The buzzer sounded and Carly was out. Destiny put in a perfect performance. Becky and Charlie were out next. I fizzed with excitement. This was, after all, my first real barrel race since leaving South Beach, where I had wiped the ring with the competition every time. I couldn't wait for my go.

Becky rounded the last barrel.

'Good luck, Spiller!' Flea grinned at me. Becky flew across the line.

Honey began with a flying start and galloped towards the first barrel. I felt a bit wobbly, but stayed focussed. The gallop was straight and long, unlike the bending and flag races. But there were three tight turns right around the barrels.

Honey slowed for the first barrel. She started to turn, light on her forehand. She pushed her weight onto her inside hind leg and turned a neat circle close to the barrel. The wobble became a slip. Before

I knew it I felt the saddle sliding and me sliding with it. I screamed, sure I would end up underneath Honey, mashed by her pounding legs or dragging along the ground. Or both!

Honey stopped dead. I hauled myself and the saddle back up onto Honey's back, moved my leg forward and lifted the saddle flap. The girth was loose at least three holes. Flea had obviously made good his threat. Idiot, I thought. I'd given him the perfect opportunity to do it while Becky and I rested our horses. I pulled the girth tighter and pushed the buckle point into the right hole with my index finger, then let the flap down and drummed my heels against Honey's sides. She sprang forward and galloped towards the second barrel, circling it tightly, then the third. We galloped back to the finish line and Flea tore away without looking at me.

Becky rushed over. Her face was pale. 'Are you okay? What happened out there?'

I shrugged. 'Just another one of Flea's personality problems.'

I slid down and watched the rest of the race from ground level. Despite everything, we placed third.

It had been an amazing day. A blue ribbon, a green ribbon against all the odds and a videotape that was worth more than any prize.

I left the ring with Becky. 'That's some trophy. Under-Twelve Champion!'

She blushed. 'It's no big deal.'

'Are you kidding? It's incredible!'

'So what happened to your *friend*?' Becky pulled a snooty Nicki King face.

I burst out laughing. 'Who knows! All dressed up and nowhere to ride.'

'Maybe she took one look at Honey in action and took off for City Stables as fast as her little chauffeur could carry her.'

Flea jumped out suddenly from behind a huge wheelie garbage bin and stood in front of us, blocking our way.

'What do you want?' I snapped.

Flea looked over his shoulder.

I glared at him. 'Well?'

'I want that tape,' he snarled.

I looked at him like he was a piece of talking doggy do. 'No.'

Flea pushed his red face closer to mine. 'If anyone

else finds out about it, you and your overgrown mongrel are history in Shady Creek.'

'I don't think so,' I said, gripping Honey's reins.

'What don't you think?' Flea sneered, mimicking me.

'If anyone else finds out about the tape, I reckon *you* will be history in Shady Creek.'

'Totally,' Becky added.

Flea went a little pale and took a step back. 'I'm warning you now. Keep your mouth shut or you'll be sorry you ever moved here.'

He turned and dragged Scud away.

Becky nudged me in the ribs. 'So will he!'

We high-fived each other, laughing, and led our champion horses back to the float.

The gymkhana was over until next year. The horses were loaded up. I pushed the bolt across the ramp and checked the tow bar. Becky was already in the car, fast asleep.

'Hey.'

I spun around. My mouth fell open. I couldn't believe what I was seeing.

'Jenna?'

She nodded. 'In the flesh.'

'What are you doing here?'

I gasped. I felt like I was going to faint right there in the mud.

'It's kind of a long story,' she said, pulling at her long fair ponytail.

It was so good to see her. I wanted to touch her to make sure she was really there. I knew I had missed her, but I hadn't realised until then how much.

'But when? How?' I stammered.

'Your parents invited me up.' She grinned. 'I heard all about the Internet horse!'

I laughed. 'Come and meet the real one.'

Jenna peeked into the float. 'She's amazing,' she said. She looked into my eyes. 'So are you. I had no idea you could ride like that.'

I scuffed at the ground with my boot.

Jenna grinned. She had braces on her teeth. 'I've got some news.'

I moaned. 'Not you, too!'

'Good news,' she laughed. 'At least, I think it is. I hope you will.'

'What?'

She took a deep breath. 'If you don't mind, I'll be staying for the summer.'

'In Shady Creek? Really?'

Jenna nodded, smiling that trademark smile. 'In Shady Creek. With you!'

I hugged her hard. 'Jenna, that's the best news!'

'And I'm getting riding lessons!'

My mouth fell open again. 'You? On a horse?'

Jenna grinned. 'I know. We're really talking devotion here!'

We laughed and hugged again.

I was definitely the luckiest kid on earth. I had my beautiful horse, two best friends and an amazing summer ahead of me.

Glossary

beanie woollen cap or hat

bikkies abbreviated form of the word "biscuits," which is the Australian term for cookies

biscuits Australian term for cookies

bitzer slang word for mongrel

brumby an Australian wild or feral horse

bunyip a mythical animal in Australian folklore, said to live in swamps and small water holes (called "billabongs")

chooks slang word for chickens

gymkhana an equestrian event, usually for young people, that involves games for riders on horses

haring to run quickly or wildly — "no haring around the paddock"

heaps lots

lamington a small, square portion of sponge cake covered in chocolate and coconut, common in Australia and New Zealand

mozzies slang abbreviation for mosquitoes

nag slang for an old or worn-out horse

RSPCA acronym for the Royal Society for the Prevention of Cruelty to Animals

swagman slang term for a transient person who roams the bush

TAB originally an acronym for "Totalisator Agency Boards," referring to outlets to place bets for Australian horse-racing

tip slang term for junkyard. To take something "to the tip" means to take it to the junkyard or the dump

titbit tidbit

torch flashlight

wriggle on telling someone to "get a wriggle on" is like telling him or her to hurry up or move faster

Acknowledgements

I would like to thank my publisher at HarperCollins, Lisa Berryman, and my editor Lydia Papandrea for their guidance and encouragement. Thank you also to the NSW Writers' Centre and Stephen Measday for their support. To my beautiful kids, Mariana, John and Simon — I love you more than I can say, thank you for being who you are. To Seb, thank you for your love, your friendship and your faith. To my family — Mum, Dad, Andy, Cassandra — thank you for my amazing horsy childhood. And thank you Clarrie — you were a truly inspirational horse.

Photo by Dyan Hallworth

KATHY HELIDONIOTIS grew up in Sydney living for the school holidays, which she spent on the New South Wales south coast studying the three essential 'Rs': reading, writing and riding (horses, of course). She now divides her time between writing stories, reading good books, teaching and looking after her three gorgeous children. Kathy has had eight children's books published so far. *Totally Horse Mad* is the first book in the Horse Mad series.

Horse Mad Summer
Book 2

I wrapped my arms around Honey's neck and hugged her hard, feeling her warmth seep into my arms and breathing her sweet horsy smell. 'Just wait,' I murmured, untacking her. 'We're going to have the best summer. The best summer ever!'

Ashleigh is itching for her Horse Mad holiday with Beck and Jenna to begin. Her two best friends will be meeting each other for the first time and she's sure all three of them will have the best summer together.

But when Jenna finally arrives from the city, Ashleigh feels like the ham in the sandwich. Torn between spending time with Jenna and helping her with her riding lessons and keeping an eye on the Creepketeers with Becky, Ashleigh's dream holiday isn't turning out as she'd hoped. The situation gets worse when Jenna confides in Ash and makes her promise not to tell anyone —.not even Becky. With the secret threatening to tear them all apart, can Ashleigh bring her two best friends together before the summer is over?